ASHLEY MCCLURE

Happily Never After

STFUARTBLAGFG

(If you know what this means, then this book is for you!)

"Can anyone be truly happy if they are not free?"

BELLE. "BEAUTY AND THE BEAST"

Contents

Acknowledgement

From the first time that read a book, I knew I wanted to be a writer one day. I loved how I could be anyone and travel anywhere sitting in a comfy chair in my room or my bed. There have been countless people who have gotten me to this place but there a a few that deserve the honor of a public thank you. So here it goes.

First to my mom and dad. They are directly responsible for the book dragon that I am today. They never made me stop reading and encouraged me anytime I spoke of being a writer.

Next is my middle school English teacher Coach Hodges. He always pushed me a little harder than everyone else and if it were not for his purple monster tests I would not roll my eyes every time I see an abbreviation for the simplest words.

Finally to my wonderful husband who not only has supported me mentally with this endeavor but has provide all of the financial backing for this to become a reality. As well as research for some of the content. I love you babe. Even still and Always will.

Five Years Ago

Vionette

It was all a lie. This whole time it was all a lie. My ears heard the words coming from the door of the bar, but my heart could not believe them. Standing in the doorway of the only bar in town, I saw my boyfriend and his friends laughing and looking at his phone.

"Read it again man! It gets me every time!"

On the screen was the message I had typed to him a few hours earlier.

"Okay. I have thought about it and tonight is the night. I think I am ready. You have been so patient, and I can see that you are struggling with waiting longer. So, I have made the decision. When you are finished with your last class, meet me in my dorm and we can finally cement this relationship. And if your kisses are any inclination of how the rest will go, I may not be able to wait for you to finish class?"

I had typed and retyped that message five times. I had never written anything like that to a guy before, never sent a dirty picture. Not even so much as a single eggplant emoji to one of my friends. I had gathered the courage and had sent my version of a sexy message, which was basically me just flirting and cussing, to him. And now they were laughing at me. He was laughing at me.

"Dude, I cannot believe you have lasted this long. But I am sure seeing a finish line makes it worth it."

"You really are a god. How have you kept this going so long?"

He laughed and put his phone back in his pocket. The same pockets I had placed my hands in while walking around the campus of The University of New Orleans. The same hands that had caressed my shoulders and my back to sleep during our movie nights in my dorm. Those hands now held my heart and squeezed.

"It hasn't been easy for sure. But I am a man of my word and I never back down from a dare. Especially when that dare looks like her! I mean no guy would give up on making her a notch in their belt!"

A dare. I was a dare. Each touch. Each kiss. Each moment of wanting to submit to the pleasure he promised. Every time he had made me question and consider giving him all of me. None of it was real. I was a game. I was a distraction. I was a fucking dare.

The tears began to fall. I felt the first one hit my chest and sink into my heart. I was moments from crumbling and then something inside me changed. I looked back at the window and the sight no longer made me want to cry. Instead there was another feeling.

Anger.

No. Not Anger.

Rage.

This was not going to happen. I made the decision standing in that doorway not to shed another tear for this monster. No, I would not give him the satisfaction of seeing me cry or crumble. I would not give anyone that power ever again. I could feel my heart being turned to stone as I stood in the doorway of what I thought my life was and what reality showed me. Men could not be trusted. Love was a lie. And I would never trust my heart to another man. This was the pact I made to myself as I turned and walked back to my dorm. Never Again.

Chapter 1

Vionette

Love doesn't exist. Fairy tales are not real. They are just something to sell condoms and chocolate. The idea that there is someone out in the big world that completes you is ridiculous. This is the mantra that plays in my head every time I open a book.

In the story, the girl is always in distress Like females as a whole are not capable of making decisions for their own lives and if they do they always fall apart. The boy is always true, honest, and noble. But all males care about is the chase, and more importantly the capture. They want the glory that comes with this magic kiss that transforms the wishes and dreams of the girl from adventure and freedom to babies and crowns. Right always wins and true love conquers all.

True love conquers nothing. The reason there is rarely a second princess movies is because it would have to show the lie. My parents had true love but it didn't save them from dying at the hands of a drunk driver my senior year of high school.

We had gone to the football game. In the south you live by the two F's. Food and football. The team had won and everyone stayed longer than we usually do. Apparently we timed it just right to share the road with Drunky Mcdrunkerston. I had a broken arm and a few dislocated ribs but my parents died on impact, once again proving that loving means loosing.

Afterwards, I went to live with my aunt in New Orleans. Aunt Margie owns an independent bookstore so, when I came to live with her it made sense that I would start working at the store. I had worked there off and on during the summertime and after school. When I started college, I just continued working there to help Aunt Margie.

The irony was not wasted on me that a girl that didn't believe in the power of love was surrounded by the greatest love stories every day. I dreamed each night as most girls do about the knight in shining armor rescuing me from a life of dullness. Granted lately the Knight in Shinning Armor had morphed into the mafia boyfriend covered in tattoos. But when the sun woke up so did I. That was never going to happen. Not for me. I made a vow five years ago that men are nothing but liars and love is just a way to break your heart. And who needs that in their life, right? I had dreamed most nights of a man with dark hair and a southern accent that would sweep me off my feet and make my heart melt with a magic kiss. I know better now. My happily ever after now consisted of finding stories before they were finished. What I want more than anything is to be an editor. As an editor, I could help shape a new generation. A generation that writes their own stories and doesn't wait to be saved. I wanted to tell a different story. A more realistic one. Love doesn't exist but pain and heartache are very real.

* * *

The day started as it usually did. I woke up. Took a quick shower. Put on a comfy pair of shorts and a sleeveless shirt. It was late summer in Louisiana. If the humidity didn't kill you the mosquitoes the size of hawks would. But I loved the city in the summer. The trees were thick with moss that hung to the ground. With each breeze they seemed to whisper secrets to those standing near them.

The daytime was full of tourists going in and out of restaurants and nursing hangovers from the night before. The night was filled with the sound of crickets and a thousand fireflies that made it seem like the stars came down to visit for a while.

I hopped on my bike and started for the store. It was about a 7 minute bike ride and a 20 minute walk but it was my favorite part of the day. Riding on the cobblestone pavement always made me smile. Not only for the good memories but the vibrations that stones made on the seat was not an unwelcome sensation. I reached the bookstore in record time and I noticed a sign hanging from the roof of the end of the building. There was an empty space that used to be a doughnut shop but the couple had retired and moved to Florida a few years ago.

"Coming Soon! Sprouts and Spice.
New Restaurant by Chef Dillon Williams."

Why did that name sound familiar? That was the chef of that fancy vegan restaurant in California that I had read about in one of the vegetarian blogs. The pictures of the food looked amazing. I had gone vegetarian a few years ago after watching a documentary about farming in the US and it was exciting to have the idea of a good vegetarian restaurant to eat at close by.

The doorbell rang as I walked inside and no sooner than the smell of books hit my nose did I hear a very familiar voice. "Hey Nettie. I just got some new releases in, can you shelve them and then redo that end shelf. Apparently aliens with five penises are the new love story. No one reads Bronte anymore."

"Sure auntie." Aunt Margie. How to describe Aunt Margie. She was tall, as were most of the people in my family. My mother's side was tall and slim. And my father's side was tall and slim. And yet I was short and curvy. Standing at a whooping 5 foot 3, my dark auburn hair and blue eyes were probably my best features although my best friend said it was my upper body. Aunt Margie was rocking the salt and pepper wicked witch in the woods look. Her entire wardrobe was from Woodstock, she was the most colorful person I had ever met. Margie knew everyone and everyone knew Margie. She never met a stranger and hers was a love story that I could believe in. She and my uncle had opened The Bookstore in the nineties and it had not changed since then. Well except for today with the addition of the alien penis. He had passed 5 years ago. Only a few months after my parents, so Aunt Margie and I had grieved together. We both lost our true loves and I could not imagine going a single day without her in it.

"How was your morning? Did you see that we will have neighbors soon? Odd that there is no picture of this chef Dillon character. But having a restaurant next door will be nice for traffic. The store could definitely use some. I don't even think people read books anymore!" I heard her mumbling all the way to the back of the store. I shook my head and let out a heavy sigh. She was not wrong. The store was in bad need of a makeover and with the invention of e Readers and Kindles, independent bookstores were becoming legends like Bigfoot or Blockbuster Video. She had tried a ton of things to drum up business for the store. She even tried a website for a little while but that went over about as much as her reading about the alien parts.

I placed my stuff down on a shelf and heard the doorbell ring again. "We are not open yet, we actually open at 8:30." I heard footsteps getting closer and when I turned around a tall man with dark hair and olive skin stood in front of me. He was wearing head to toe black and a silver chain around his neck. He had honey-colored eyes and full lips. He looked as if sin had become a person. At least 6 feet tall and had a body that would make Hercules jealous. I was trying to form a coherent sentence and then a silky voice said, "That is OK. I am not here for a book. Who reads anymore anyway? I am here to introduce myself. I saw you walking in from the parking lot, and I thought I have to know who this angel is. So, I followed you in." I melted for a moment and then found my brain again.

I took a breath, crossed my arms which did little to hide the ample chest that was also uncharacteristic of my family and simply said "no."

"No. What does that mean?" He actually looked stunned. No, that wasn't right. He looked interested and maybe a little stunned.

"It means no. I am not going to give my name. It means no you do not need to know who I am. It means no I am no angel. And it means no you have no chance in hell of me caring who you are. I can help you with a book but as you said you don't need that so have a great day."

The stranger laughed. I could not help but be intrigued by

the timber in his voice. He was a book boyfriend come to life. Focus.

"Wow. Who pissed in your coffee this morning babe? I am just trying to be friendly. We are going to be neighbors after all."

Against my better judgment, curiosity got the better of me and I asked "What do you mean neighbors?"

"Me and my best friend are opening the restaurant next door. So, get used to this face, girly. You will be seeing it a lot."

This could not be the vegetarian chef. He would be kind. Anyone who has morals would be kind, right? He would not objectify women. "What did you say your name was again," I asked him just to confirm my suspicion and waited hoping I was correct. There was no way this cocky self centered man was Dillon Williams.

"I didn't say it but I'm glad you are interested now. It's Max. Maximilian Chase." A sigh of relief left before I could stop it. "Oh. So you are not Dillon Williams?"

He smiled a smile that can only be described as the smile a cat would have right before catching a mouse and leaned on the desk. "No, I most definitely am not. But if it meant getting your number, I could be whoever you want me to be."

Ick.

The cringe that ran through my body was instant. This was exactly the reason that I had sworn not to have anything to do with the opposite sex. The goal was always the same. It was all about the chase.

I chuckled a little bit. "You could be Prince Harry himself and you would not get my number." I said it with as much gumption as I could muster but even when I used my "big girl voice" as Charlotte called it, it still came out like a little kid insulting a friend on the playground. I had only ever succeeded in telling someone off successfully once five years ago but that was in my head. Did that count? Sure it counts. Right? Anyone can be anyone over the phone. In person I became an anxious blabber. The more stress in a situation the more my mouth would spew the dumbest things.

"Tough room. OK well I hope that your day gets better, and you find some customer service before an actual customer comes in. Although by the looks of the dust on the books that doesn't happen often." Max smiled with the wit of his insult.

"Young man. If all you are here for is to bash my store and make my niece uncomfortable then you have succeeded in both, and I would ask you to leave now." Margie didn't sound like a child on a playground. She sounded more like a retired drill sergeant that now deals with unruly prisoners every day. Max straightened. He apologized to aunt Margie and then winked at me before he left the same way he had come in.

"Well, he was an ass. But a good looking one. I will give him that."

"Aunt Marge. Gross."

"Just because I am old doesn't mean I am blind child. That boy was smooth as a pond first thing in the morning. And just as shallow if I had to bet. Was that the chef you were gushing about?" Margie wiggled her eyebrows and made a clicking noise.

"No. I guess he was attractive if you notice that kind of thing. But I don't. Men are trouble and you know I swore them off a long time ago. Besides, I have the best boyfriend right here." I gestured to one of the books on the shelves and wiggled my eyebrows. These men were always dependable, reliable, predictable.

"Those are not gonna keep you warm at night or hold you when you're upset. You cannot share a life with a book. I won't be here forever, and I want to know that you are taken care of by something flesh and blood, preferably with only one set of male genitalia. You need someone to run the store with. I had 60 years with your uncle, and I would not trade it for anything. We built this store with our bare hands and filled it with the greatest love stories of all time. Including our own."

Margie hugged me in one of her bear hugs that just made you melt. She kissed my head and then walked away leaving me wondering what a love that strong and true would feel like. I loved my aunt and the legacy that she had built here. But this is not my legacy. The bookstore was a beautiful dream, but that dream was Margie's. I dreamed of being an editor. There was one place in the city not too far from the spot that I stood in that could make my dream come true. My best friend Charlotte started working there in her junior year of college to help cover expenses. I had wanted to apply but felt guilty for leaving Margie high and dry at the store. So I changed my status to full time here and never pursued it further. Except in my dreams. In my dreams, Angela Fields was asking me to run an office for her in New York. The doorbell rang with the first customer, and I snapped back to reality. Dreams don't come true and happily ever after is a lie. But I could not help but smile a little at the confidence that the strangers words gave me. Maybe men were good for somethings?

Chapter 2

Will

How the hell does anything get done in this city? Its like time went back 20 years. When I decided to open this restaurant I had several different places in mind. I could have picked Dallas. But I left and stayed gone for a reason. I could have chosen California. That would have been a good one. There was definitely a big market for Vegan restaurants there, but there was also the beach and I was not a beach person. I could have stayed in New York but with a new restaurant opening almost every weekend, I wanted a place to create my own brand. Not the one that my partner wanted but my own. I needed his financial backing but I did not need him looking over my shoulder. I know this business inside and out.

I had a dream to have a place that fused high cuisine with reasonable prices for all pallets. Unfortunately dreams cost money. And when researching places New Orleans was by far the cheapest real estate. It also has a love for food built right into the people and the city. So I grabbed my best friend and we made the move south. Max and I met at Culinary school. He was running from his fathers money and decided that becoming a chef would really piss him off. I was running from a past of juvenile court and anger management problems. We hit it off the moment we met and never looked back. When I told him about my idea his only response was "How do the girls look in New Orleans?"

"I am not sure but with a state motto of 'let the good times roll' they cannot be bad right?"

It was not surprising that Max would base this entire decision on the caliber of women he would have to choose from. Neither of us were big on relationships. With the hours that a chef keeps its hard to meet women. That's not true. Its very easy, make a vegetarian salad and they practically throw themselves at you. They fall for the food and the status but then the long nights get old and they leave. I decided that the 'friends with benefits' role was best without the friend part. And there had never been a girl to challenge my view on this. I knew that Max would be leaving a trail of broken hearts when we moved. But I would be leaving expectations and control.

I have been in the restaurant business for several years now. Always needing partners and financiers, so I was never able to have my own restaurant. It wasn't a bad setup. I could have free reign for the food and the atmosphere. But it wasn't mine. I wanted something that was mine. I had some savings from my parents when they divorced, saved for a rainy day but I could never pull the trigger and it wasn't enough. So when we bought this place I used the father of an old friend who was looking into getting into the restaurant business. He did mostly hedge funds and tech start ups but we talked and he liked the idea of a business in the 'Big Easy' and here we are.

I loved this place the moment we got off the plane. Finding a space was not difficult, and the process of buying was a breeze. There was something to be said about southern hospitality after all. It needed a lot of work but it was next to a bookshop that had charm. And looked like it had been there for quite some time.

I pretty much lived at the restaurant, and rarely ventured out using Max as an errand boy. I sent him for breakfast one day and he returned with coffee and beignets.

"It's about time. I am starving! They better be warm?"

"They are hot but not as hot as the girl that works next door. Jesus. I have seen some lookers but this one puts them all to shame."

"You say that about every girl. I am sure she is just the normal pretty and your mind is just clouded cause you haven't been laid in a week!"

"True. I haven't and I may be a little clouded but I'm telling you, this girl is something special. I tried to talk to her but she told me no. Then I told her that we are neighbors and she got all intense wanting to know if I was Dillon Williams. I told her that I wasn't and she shut me down again. I even used a smolder smile and nothing. Which I think made me fall in love even more. I'm telling you man. You have to see this girl. Just go over and introduce yourself. She seemed interested in Dillon Williams after all."

"I don't need a distraction right now. I am trying to get this place ready for opening in two weeks and from the look of it I am doing it alone. So thanks but no thanks."

"Your loss dude. What do you say we have an actual dinner tonight and scope out the restaurant scene in this town.

Besides, you are getting fat!"

"Just because I don't have a 12 pack doesn't mean I'm fat! Dad bods are trending right now." I smiled at my comeback.

"You wish! So shall I make a reservation for tonight?"

"Yes, but you're paying. These beignets are cold."

"Deal."

Chapter 3

Vionette

After a long day of nothing really, I got home around five o'clock and my phone began ringing. I looked at the name and rolled my eyes as I hit the little green button knowing the voice on the other end before she even started talking.

"Hey Bitch. Get Dressed. Something slutty. We are going out and I am not taking no for an answer. You have been working at that store too much. You need to let your hair down. I'll be there at 7. I made a reservation for 7:30 for dinner before we go make bad decisions! Love ya."

Charlotte Piper. Best friends since freshman year, Charlotte is the gas to my brakes. I have curves but in the wrong places. Charlotte has everything in the right place. She has a body that defies all laws of physics. Her eyes are a piercing blue and she has long dirty-blonde hair. Charlotte was the stuff of every boy's wet dream and every woman's worst nightmare. While I made a pact to swear off men, Charlotte had made a pact to collect them all. I knew that a night with Charlotte meant crowded bars and sweaty men. But I was hungry, and Charlotte would not take no for an answer.

Giving up on the desire to get into comfy clothes and heat up a hot pocket as I read, I gathered my supplies to try and make myself presentable. I curled my hair, found my black dress, and made myself ready for being whisked away to bad music but the best company. At least until Charlotte found her catch of the night and I could slip away.

Charlotte arrived right on time wearing a dress that would make Jessica Rabbit blush. Bright red with a slit on both sides that left little to the imagination. Her hair was down and in loose waves, making her look like she just stepped out of Hustler Magazine. I immediately felt self-conscious. I was wearing a black dress that I wore each time we went out. Charlotte had made me purchase it for just such occasions.

"Every woman needs a little black dress. A woman can rule the world with the right little black dress," she had proclaimed when she saw it on the rack. Spaghetti strapped to hold my boobs in place, the dress hugged every single curve as if it had been made just for me. A small slit on the right leg that showed just enough skin when I walked and a little too much when I sat down. Which is why I always wore black spandex shorts underneath.

"You look amazing Char, as always." I looked into the face of my best friend unable to help the comparison that was happening.

"No. Nettie you look stunning. I forgot you were hiding those under those baggy shirts." She motioned to my chest. "I have to wear a push up bra to get half that cleavage." I knew she was lying but that was Charlotte. No matter how I felt about myself, Char always made me feel like I was the most beautiful woman in the room. This was my fairy tale. This was the love I could believe in. We met freshman year in English lit. I was the aspiring editor and Char the party girl looking for an easy degree. Charlotte was the one who pulled me up from the bottom. She was the voice that made me feel worthy of anyone's time again. Her personality was enough to make me fall in love with her, and her being there for me and never giving up on me made us soul mates.

"Let's go! I made reservations and I don't want to be late. They will give away your table if you are even a minute late. And I am trying to not be a bitch today. Well, starting now."

"Okay. I am ready, I just have to grab my bag." I reached for my large bag and Charlotte gasped.

"Why are you bringing that? Are you planning on robbing the place?"

"No. I want to make sure I have everything I could need." Most of the things I needed in this bag was for her sake. Tylenol and a Gatorade for after the club: a shirt for when she spilled or barfed all over herself. And then my book of course for if I could find a quiet-ish place to read. I didn't do the club scene. Having random strangers buy me drinks and grope me all night was not my thing. I gripped the bag tighter knowing Charlotte would snatch it out of my hands to inspect what was inside.

Just as I tightened my hold, Charlotte grabbed the bag. "You have got to be fucking with me. You are not seriously taking a book to a dance club? Really. Have I taught you nothing? The point of tonight is to live life in front of you. You cannot spend your whole life looking down. Look up for a change. You're missing some pretty great things.

I grabbed the book and placed it back in the bag and said "I may be missing things but those things don't matter to me. I like my books. They don't hurt. They don't disappoint. Well, some do but that isn't my point. Books are predictable."

Charlotte sighed and placed her arm around me. "I know that you still have issues from that which won't be named, but you are a beautiful, intelligent, vibrant woman. I don't want to see you waste this…" She waved her hand up and down my curves. "…on books that won't appreciate it. You need something flesh and blood."

I scrunch my eyebrows. "You sound like Margie. She told me the same thing right before telling me that she wants me to run the store when she is done." I laughed but it wasn't a carefree laugh. Far from it. It was a laugh that held the weight of expectation. I was expected to take over The Bookstore when Margie retired. That had always been the plan. Though who came up with the plan I am not sure.

"Well, you don't have to figure that all out tonight. Tonight is for making bad decisions. Tonight is for getting into trouble of the best kind." Charlotte knew how to bring me back to the here and now, and I loved her for it.

"So grab your loser purse and let's go. I wasn't kidding when I said that they would give our table away. And it will be your fault if we lose it because of this stupid suitcase." We both laughed as we made our way down the stairs of the building. And when the warm humid air hit my bare skin I could not shake the feeling that something was going to be different tonight.

Chapter 4

Will

I was right in the middle of inventory when my phone lit up and the familiar text notification pierced the silence of the storage room. I pulled it out of my pocket and looked at the screen. My financial partner Mark Price. He had financed a few of the projects that I had done since graduating from culinary school.

Price- "I hope that everything is on track still?"

Me- "Yeah. I am fighting deliveries taking a little longer than I am used to. Why didn't you warn me that I was setting up shop in a time machine. Seriously. Its like 1990 here."

Price- "I am sure that you will get it figured out. Welcome to Louisiana where the speech is fast and the work is slow. Its not called "The Big Easy" for nothing."

Me- "I promise we will have everything ready for next week."

Price- "Just make sure to take a break every once in a while. I am sure Max will be more than helpful in that department."

Me- "Yes. He is already planning for us to check out the local restaurant scene this evening."

Price- "I am sure that he is wanting to check out more than just the restaurants. Enjoy. I will be in town for the opening."

Me- "I'll keep in touch till then."

I put the phone back in my pocket noting the time as I did so. I needed to get ready for the big night with Max. He was a lot of things but late was not one of them especially when food and the possibility of meeting his next great love was on the table.

I walked the two miles back to my place. It wasn't much but it was comfortable. Certainly not the modern bachelor pad that I was used to having in New York. The building that I had picked was purely for distance purposes. But it had a lot of charm. Totally brick from all sides. It was a duplex and the older couple that lived next to me was a fairy tale come to life.

I walked the steps and saw the gentleman sitting in his rocking chair on the small shared porch. I smiled at the fact that people did actually sit on their porches here and sip sweet tea.

"Hey Mr. Walsh. How are you and the misses doing this evening?" I turned to place the key in the door.

"Faire le bein young man. Still this side of da grass so I canno complain to much."

"I have never thought of it that way before but I guess that is true?" Understanding this accent was a skill I was still working on. I could not help but smile at the old man.

I walked inside and placed my keys on the key holder next to the door. I decided I had enough time to send a few quick emails and then shower. I had some messages from old flings from New York and a few from vendors that I had met here in New Orleans. But unlike Max, I saw women as a distraction. Don't get me wrong at the right time they could be fun and I was a red blooded man with needs and wants. But most women don't like coming in second to a building. And I never knew where the wind would blow me for the next venture so I kept my relationship status uncomplicated.

I finished my shower refreshed and renewed. I put on a dark navy suit that my mother had given me on the opening of my first restaurant. It was somewhat of a lucky suit if you believed in superstition like that. I had never had a business deal go wrong when wearing it. So I figured for my first introduction to the new city it could not hurt to have a little luck on my side. I gave myself one more glance in the mirror and then walked out the door. I put the key in the door to lock it and a hand hit my shoulder.

Instinct took over and I grabbed the hand and twisted pinning the wrist to their back in one fluid motion.

"Hey man. Its me. Max."

"I have told you a million times not to sneak up on me. Remember the bloody nose from last year?" I let go of his arm

"Yeah. I had to throw that shirt away. Could not get the stains out."

"You should learn from your mistakes friend."

"Probably but then where is the fun in that?" He gave me his smolder smile and I could not help but see what the girls saw when they looked at my best friend.

"I picked a great place for us to try. Came highly recommended by the lady who owns the bookshop next door. I went back in to see if I could get another look at her niece. I am telling you man. Beautiful doesn't even begin to describe her. I thought she has that whole 'innocent bookworm' thing going on and then she opened her mouth and insulted me nine ways to Tuesday and it went straight to my dick and I haven't been able to stop thinking about her. I think I found my next target."

"Everything goes straight to your dick. Why don't we worry about getting the restaurant done. I don't need you leaving me every five minutes to go have sex with a townie and then leaving me to do all the work. Besides, she will end up being just another story for you to tell your ego when you eventually met your match."

"No man. I am telling you. Something about this chick is different."

"Sure. Whatever you say." How many times had I heard that line? Countless.

We got in the Uber and started the 10 minute drive to the other side of the city. It was not uncommon for Max to fixate on a certain girl and make it his challenge. But he actually seemed a little rattled by this mystery girl. I could not deny that part of me was curious about the woman who could rattle Max this much. Any girl that could do that was worth meeting in person. So I made a mental note to drop by the bookstore tomorrow and introduce myself and see if this girl was all that Max said she was or if she was just another distraction.

Chapter 5

Vionette

"I told you! If we hadn't had to talk about your stupid book then we would have been on time and we would be double fisting dirty martinis right now." Charlotte was fuming. She was always right. Even when she was wrong, she was right. And now standing in the hot humid air, I wished she had been wrong.

"Sorry for making us late Char. I will pay for dinner! Just don't be mad at me please. I am sure we can find somewhere else to eat. This place isn't that good for the money anyway."

Wrong.

In true Charlotte fashion she had picked one of the best restaurants in the city and conveniently forgot she was late to my apartment and late because of dissing my bag. I hated her being mad at me even if it made no sense that she was. So I hoped I could play on Charlotte's cheap side. As much as she liked to party, she liked to party for free even more.

"I wanted to eat here. I made reservations here." The other thing about Charlotte Piper is she doesn't like change. She is a type A planner and there is only plan A. I cringed and then sweetened the deal by offering to pay for drinks once we got to the dance club. I didn't have the money at all but that felt like a problem for two hours from now. Right now my mission was to keep Charlotte from making a scene and still be my friend by the end of the evening.

More and more people were rushing in and out of the restaurant. And from the corner of my eye I thought someone was waving to us. My suspicions were confirmed when Charlotte said, "Um Net. I think that god sitting at that table is waving to you?" I turned and my stomach dropped. Max, the prick from this morning was waving for us to come over. He was once again in all black but this time a suit and tie, and he was not alone. Another man clad in a navy suit was sitting opposite him. All I could see of him was that he had broad shoulders, from his height in the chair he was tall. Not slim but fit. Like the kind of body that likes tacos and weight training. His dark hair was swept back with some pieces falling to what I assumed was an average face. His face was buried in the menu.

Charlotte grabbed my arm with a little more force than was necessary and said while smiling, "Do you know that hunk of man meat? And if so, how and why have you not said something about him!" Charlotte started to fix her dress and used the window to fix her hair.

"I don't know him. He followed me into the bookstore this morning and I immediately kicked him out. He is a grade a prick, Char. Trust me." Charlotte continued to look in the direction and she seemed to want to actually go over there. Then I found myself being pulled to the table. "Let's go say hello. He cannot be that bad and no one makes a good impression before 9 o'clock am. Besides we need a table and they are sitting at a table for four. Its fate babe."

Charlotte and I reached the table and Charlotte immediately took over the conversation. "Hello handsome. I know every beautiful face in the town, and I have never seen yours. I'm Charlotte. And you are?" Standing slightly behind her, my mouth hanging open, I looked at my friend in awe. Charlotte could command any room and any man for that matter. She had confidence to spare and most would come across as being conceited but not on her. On her it just made her seem more desirable. Max immediately looked her up and down, but the stranger with the menu didn't move. He just started at the menu as if he would be given a test on it later.

Standing from the table, Max reached for Charlotte's hand and placed a kiss on her knuckle, "My name is Max. And I am at your service beautiful. Your every wish is my command." I could not help the face that I made at the oily response. I am sure you could hear the eye roll that I gave Max, but when I looked at my friend, Charlotte was eating it up.

"Really. I could really use a table here. You think we could join you and your.......?"

I looked at the stranger. His face was still buried in the menu, and he hadn't made a sound. "This is Will, my partner. We are new in town and wanted to check out the local restaurants. This one came highly recommended by Yelp and I am starting to see why. If the food is half as delicious as you two ladies then I am never eating anywhere again."

"Oh, that is fantastic. We love a good bromance. I guess it is true that all the good-looking ones are gay. And great line by the way.I actually felt something just then." She laughed as she said it and sat down, dropping the seductive act immediately.

Max spit out his water and quickly said, "What? No, not that kind of partner, business partner. I assure you that I am not gay. I am as straight as a board. In fact, if you play this evening well, I can show you exactly how straight I can be."

Ick again.

My gag reflex was about to make an introduction of its own because of this man and also because my friend was enjoying it.

"Well, Max. If you play your cards right, I may take you up on that offer." Charlotte picked the art of seduction right back up. As well as the menu that had been dropped off, without me even realizing it.

I grabbed her wrist under the table. "Charlotte, they are clearly having a boys night or whatever this is. Lets just go find another restaurant." I was in no mood to watch the two of them play seduction tonight. I wanted to eat and then find a booth at the club and forget that I am there until I can sneak out and go back home to my current book boy toy.

"I would hate to see you two go but I am sure that I would enjoy watching you leave." Max never looks at me when he says it and Charlotte just leans into him more eating up every word that he says.

Before I can give him a piece of my mind about how he should be treating women if he wants to make a good impression a voice stops me.

"I guess I should just leave. Maxi you seem to be in good hands and I would like to keep my dinner in my stomach."

Holy Shit.

That tone.

That accent.

Both unfamiliar and all too familiar. I looked to my left and was not met with the first page of the menu. I was met with the most beautiful face I had ever seen. A man had only rendered me speechless one other time. And after that I swore never again to trust lust. My heart rate picked up. My breathing increased. My palms become sweaty. This man was my dream come true. Dark hair lazily swept out of his face with a few strands rebelling against the hair gel. Full lips that looked like they held every temptation to bring me to ruin in a single word. But what I noticed the most was his eyes. One brown and one green. Like the dirt after a rain and the sea after a storm. He wore a white shirt under a tailored navy suit that fit him well. No tie and the top two buttons were undone. So he liked to be more casual. While Max gave an heir of money, Will gave an heir of work. His hands looked worn. And I noticed a small band aid on his left hand. He had a voice that could melt butter and his accent was like lightning running straight to my core.

I was familiar with that accent as it was also the accent that belonged to him. Five years ago I met what I thought was my dream guy. He was tall and handsome. With light brown hair, and green eyes. He was the kind of boyfriend that any girl would love to have. He was from Dallas originally and came from money. His father financed new businesses and had a hand in almost everything you could imagine. Matthew was a business major and we had bonded over mutual life paths. Both of us were expected to take over the family business. I had planned a life with him. I had planned to have a family. He was my first love, my first French kiss and if not for a night outside a bar he would have been my first EVERYTHING. Just hearing that twang put me right back in that doorway.

"Sure thing man. Whatever you want to do! See ya tomorrow.

I will be late." Max didn't even look away from Charlotte and she said, "Nettie you were just saying how you wanted to go home right. I think I will be fine with Max here. Right Max?" Max smiled a predatory smile that Charlotte answered with her own.

"Yeah, I was just saying that. Let me know when you get home." A heavy sigh left my lips. I had expected to be ditched at some point in the evening, but I didn't think that I would be stood up before at least having a meal.

I grabbed my bag and stood. Before I could completely stand my chair was moving behind me and a strong hand was placed on my lower back.

"Let me help you. As we are both being discarded to the wolves this evening." The stranger helped me up and then slid the chair back under the table. Max and Charlotte didn't even blink.

Chapter 6

Vionette

I was dressed up and hungry and neither of those had a solution that I could see. Not to mention that I had left my ride gazing into the eyes of a creep. My stomach growled so loud that I was sure anyone within a few feet could hear it. The night was at least nice and the fireflies had begun to light the sky. I could not help but think how beautiful the city was. That feeling didn't last long.

"I should apologize for my friend. He is a good guy but can be an ass when he sees something he wants and apparently your friend is the target of the evening." That voice again. Apparently, I was not alone on the sidewalk. I turned to face the stranger once more. The man was intimidating sitting down. Standing up he was downright terrifying. He had to be over six feet tall. Not quite a "dad bod" but not the herculean body of his friend, and the suit he was wearing suggested he had money, but his hands suggested he didn't mind putting in a hard day's work. Maybe he liked rock climbing. I had heard that many rich men do outdoor activities to keep them 'grounded.'

"No need to apologize for anything. Charlotte is the same way. I am used to being discarded once she finds her conquest for the evening. I just thought I would have a full stomach before getting ditched. Have a good night." I was in no mood to have even a remotely civil conversation with anyone. The current status of the evening was making me even more uninterested in having a conversation with this person. Especially since my body was not getting that hint. It wasn't just the way that he spoke. He smelled of spice and rain. For some reason that was familiar but I could not place it. I turned around to start walking home, wanting nothing more than to eat a hot pocket and get out of this stupid dress but stopped after I heard that voice again.

"I know a good BBQ place around the corner if you would like to join me? " He was standing with his hands in his pockets. Everything about him oozed raw sexuality. It was like he was my own brand of heroine. Cooked in a lab for the sole purpose to distract me from my goals. Though what those goals were, I had no idea. My stomach growled again and I remembered the goal. What was this guy's deal. Had he met a voodoo priestess and been given a charm that he placed on me when he gently guided me from the seat?

I turned to fully face him. "I am fine. I don't live too far away and my Uber is right around the corner. She may have ditched me but Charlotte is the poster girl for making it right.

"I don't eat BBQ. I don't eat meat. I am a vegetarian. Good night."

I turned again and started to walk. I felt a warm calloused

hand grab my wrist. Without thinking I turned and threw my weight into a right hook that Apollo Creed would be proud of. My knuckles made contact and then my brain registered what had happened. Will grabbed his nose, red starting to stain his fingers.

"Oh My God! I am so sorry. It was a reflex. I took a few self-defense classes in college, and I guess I paid better attention than I thought I did. Holy shit! Are you OK? That is a lot of blood. Do you need me to call an ambulance or the police? Wait, don't call the police. I am not cut out for jail. I am so sorry. Why did you grab my arm like that?"

"Jesus lady. I was trying to be nice. I think you broke my nose. And I am not gonna call the cops. Besides I don't have a name to tell them. What would the report be? *Yes, officer I was trying to eat a nice dinner and then I got booted out because my best friend met a girl and the girl kicked her friend out. When I tried to make sure the lady got home OK, she turned into Mike Tyson and here we are.'"

That accent made him attractive despite the blood covering his hands and the front of his shirt. He could take a punch even if it was thrown by a girl. And I was into the whole gangster, bad guy vibe in my reading lately. Sure. That was it. My inner self just registered him as the current book boyfriend and that was it. That was the reason my entire body was betraying me at just the sound of his voice.

"Vionette." I made myself remember my manners. Probably should have done that before throwing the punch but here we are.

"Is that some Cajun swear word?"

"No. It's my name. Vionette Boudreaux."

I looked in my bag and found the T-shirt and gave it to him.

He took it from my hands with a look of confusion but no hesitation.

"Thanks. And that is one hell of a name. I'm Will. Nice to meet you." He extended his hand for a handshake, and it was covered in red, so he pulled it back to rest on his nose once again. "I don't mean to pry but why do you have a t- shirt in your bag? Planning to add bank robbery to your assault charge this evening?" He was both kidding and also a little concerned.

I looked back at him. A little amused but also angry that he thought I would be capable of such a thing. "No! And I didn't assault you. You grabbed me. I was acting in self-defense. As for the shirt, my friend in there has as much self-control as she does tactfulness. So this is for when she gets sick and throws up on everything. A walk of shame is a little better when you cannot see the effects of your poor decisions. Speaking of poor decisions, you are covered in blood. Are you sure you are okay?"

"Yeah. The nose bleeds like a son of a bitch and makes it look worse than what it is. It's not the first time I have been punched in the nose and it certainly won't be that last. And besides, it's not every day that you get punched by a girl in a dress like that." He looked down over the edge of the shirt. Heat flooded my cheeks before I could stop it.

Did he really think flirting and holding my shirt while covered in blood; blood that he had because I had punched him, was a good idea? He had balls. No stop. Why was I thinking about his balls? I wanted nothing to do with his balls. Or any other part of him.

"Keep telling yourself that." My inner voice had apparently chosen anarchy.

"Clearly you are in no more need of my service. Hope you

have a great rest of your life Will. Oh, and keep the shirt." I left him on the sidewalk, but I could not escape the fact that two men in one day had both reinforced my resolve to swear off men. Even if this one had made me think things long forgotten.

* * *

My apartment greeted me with the same quiet as before and I changed out of the dress. I brushed my teeth and grabbed a book. Weirdly I was not hungry. At least not for food. I did, however, find an overwhelming desire to find out what happened with the girl and her mobster boyfriend that I had been reading for the last few days. I cuddled in with a nice cup of tea and continued Annabel's story…

As she turned the corner, she was forced into the arms of the very person she was trying to run from. She had been in a cage her whole life. She had finally tasted freedom and vowed never to be locked away again. Even if that cage came with some pretty good percs. The mind numbing orgasms being at the top of that list. She wanted nothing to do with this guy and his percs. She wanted her freedom. To finally be able to make her own decisions and not be told what she was going to do. She wanted to be free of the expectations that were placed on her just because of her last name. Yes her family was a big deal. They had controlled the entire west side of Brooklyn for the last 20 years. This marriage had been a truce between her family and the O'Shae family of the east side. But she was more than a truce. She as a person and she was going to prove it one way or the other. Starting with getting away from Nail O'Shae and this house.

35

I stopped reading and looked at the clock and it read 2:55 am. I dreaded sleep because I knew that I would hear that voice and see those eyes as soon as mine closed.

Chapter 7

Will

I had been punched before but never that efficiently and never by someone who looked like her. I had a very different vision of how this night was going to go. Max and I would have a nice meal. He would go to the club and find a random girl to hook up with. I would go back to the restaurant and get some more work done and then pass out in the manager's office like every other night. But the replay of what happened continued to play in my head.

"Oh My God! I am so sorry. It was a reflex. I took a few self-defense classes in college, and I guess I paid better attention than I thought I did. Holy shit! Are you OK? That is a lot of blood. Do you need me to call an ambulance or the police? Wait, don't call the police. I am not cut out for jail. I am so sorry, but I did warn you that I had a good right hook. Why did you grab my arm like that?"

"Jesus lady. I was trying to be nice. I think you broke my

nose. And I am not gonna call the cops. Besides I don't have a name to tell them. What would the report be? 'Yes, officer I was trying to eat a nice dinner and then I got booted out because my best friend met a girl and the girl kicked her friend out and then when I tried to make sure the lady got home OK. She turned into Mike Tyson and here we are.'"

I was not mad at her. In fact I was impressed. It was a good punch. She clearly could handle herself. I was still trying to get my nose to stop bleeding. The pain was making me see double. Though seeing two of her was like a fantasy come to life. She had said her name while reaching into her bag and all I could think was how much I hoped it wasn't pepper spray.

"Is that some kind of Cajun cuss word?"

"No, it's my name." She said it as if me asking her what she said was making her night unbearable. I was the one that got punched. She handed me what looked to be a band t-shirt.

Why did she have other clothes in her bag? This girl was a mystery that I needed to solve. Yes that was all this was. It had nothing to do with the fact that she was beautiful. Just as Max had described her. Beautiful was not the right word. But with the pounding headache and blurred vision I could not come up with anything better.

"You are covered in blood. Are you sure you are Okay?"

"Yeah. The nose bleeds like a son of a bitch and makes it look worse than what it is. It's not the first time I have been punched in the nose and it certainly won't be that last. And besides, it's not every day that you get punched by a girl in a dress like that." My vision was finally getting a little clearer. Damn. Beautiful was definitely not the right word. She had dark auburn hair. The kind that you think is brown but in the sunlight you can see the red. She was a good bit shorter than me. If I hugged her she would probably fit right under my chin if I leaned down. She was curvy in all the right places. But lean like she was maybe a runner or swimmer. She was wearing a black dress that fit those curves perfectly. I could not stop the image of my hands tracing those curves. Both with and without the dress. I could not tell what color her eyes were but if I had to guess I would say hazel or blue maybe. I was looking at her over the top of the shirt. Her cheeks were flushed and it made her even more attractive.

She said something about her dress and then the next thing I know she is walking away. And if the front view was good, the back was my undoing. She had the most perfect ass I had ever seen. I was worried she was going to be a distraction for Max and it seemed I needed to worry about her being a distraction for myself.

I wanted to follow after her but I had some semblance of self preservation. After all, I don't chase after the girls. The girls chase me. The fact that my best friend was currently trying to score with her best friend also helped with keeping me rooted to my current spot. I had bigger problems right now. I was covered in blood. I was hungry. And I was intrigued by this girl that just punched me in the nose. It was going to be a long night.

I headed back to the my restaurant which was a three mile walk from my current location according to my app. Nothing helped work off steam better than hard labor. That and some good food.

I stopped at the BBQ place I had mentioned. I had my own place but this was easier. I had a cot in the managers office and kept a change of clothes there just in case. Once I finished my meal I started on sanding the table tops for the tables.

With each pass of the sander, my mind wandered to another set of curves. This was going to be a long night.

Chapter 8

Vionette

Pleasantly surprised, I did not dream of the tall dark and handsome stranger. In fact, I didn't dream at all. My alarm woke me up at the usual six am like normal. But I didn't feel normal. Could it be? Was I upset that I didn't dream of Will? No, that is ridiculous. I had met him one time. We had one conversation and I punched him in the nose for Christ's sake. Even if I hadn't sworn off guys for life, I would not have given Will the time of day. With a bloody nose he still thought he had a shot. Guys with that kind of ego were just the kind that made me swear them off to begin with. Bloody and battered, he still was committed to the chase. Still, something was different.

I donned my bike and rode to the store. I passed many trash cans with the influences of bad decisions from the night before. I walked into the bookstore assuming I would find Aunt Margie complaining about some teenager coming into the store asking for the cliff notes of The Scarlet Letter. Instead, I saw Max carrying a very large and heavy box with Margie directing him where to go.

"Just put it next to those others. That will be Nettie's task when she arrives. Punishment for treating our new neighbor so poorly." I could have sworn Margie yelled that last sentence knowing I had walked in the door. "I know I taught her how to treat new people, especially new people who look like you. Why if I was thirty years younger I would…"

"Why are you here Max?" I yelled the first thing to come to my head. I did not want my aunt to finish that sentence. For everyone's sake. "I trust you had a good evening with Charlotte last night." I folded my arms and glared at the man bending down. He was more casually dressed this time in a black shirt and gray sweat pants shorts. Somehow this looked made him look even better than the suit did. I could not help but glance at his butt while doing so. Like him or not the man was built well. How two men entered my little world in 24 hours and both were beautiful was a mystery. Maybe the universe was testing my nerve to see how committed I was to the pact that I had made.

"I had a perfectly lovely time. Thank you so much for allowing me the pleasure of stealing her away from you. She is a remarkable young woman. But I guess it takes one to know one."

I laughed. "Are you saying that you too are a remarkable young woman?"

Max's stare met mine and he looked amused. As much as he annoyed me, he was easy to talk to.

"I believe he was paying you a compliment. She is your friend after all. Like calls to like. That sort of thing. And stop insulting my helper this morning. Having some male energy in this place is a welcome change. Be nice!" That last command almost made me vomit when I looked at the grin on Max's face.

"You heard her. Be nice." The last part came out as whisper as he passed me to place the box down next to an empty shelf. A small part of me somewhere deep inside my stomach, and a little further down, reacted to the brush of air next to my ear and the timber in his voice even with a whisper. . I guess I could not blame Charlotte to much for ditching me for him last night.

"I would but no. You stole my friend, my date, and my meal last night. You owe me. Besides, it's early. I guess the date with Char didn't go as well as you mentioned?" I turned to start preparing for the day and heard heavy footsteps close behind me.

"It was great. We ate. We drank. We danced. We had amazing sex but then she just left. She didn't want to cuddle or talk. She said she had an early morning and had to get back. I was prepared to give her that line but she used it on me first. I have never had that happen and it's honestly messing with my brain. You are her best friend. Which is why I am here. She didn't leave me a way to contact her." He looked hurt. He genuinely looked hurt. Yet another fly in Charlotte's web.

"Are you sure you are not a remarkable woman? No man ever asks those questions. You definitely don't seem like the type to do so. Maybe it didn't go as well as you thought. Maybe she left because you didn't measure up." I regretted the words as soon as I heard them. But I fixed my face with cold indifference.

Max put his hand to his chest as if he were clutching an imaginary string of pearls. "And here I was hoping that you would help a broken man when he is down. Harsh bro! I guess you are not going to give me her number then?" He gave me what I can only assume was his version of puppy dog eyes but it came across as more o f a sexy sad face.

"No. Charlotte does what she wants. If she didn't want to give you her number then I am sure she had a good reason." I was not in the mood to play matchmaker. Nor was I in the mood to feel Charlotte's anger toward me for the second time in two days.

"Well, then I guess she would not want this invitation to the opening of the restaurant. And I so happen to have one for you also. Your aunt mentioned you were very interested in the opening but I don't remember why."

I could care less about this man hooking up with my best friend again, but I was very interested in finding out more about this restaurant and the mysterious Dillon Williams. I tried googling him the first time I saw the banner, but could not find a single picture. I did find that he grew up in Dallas, Texas and that he had completed culinary school there with Max. I also saw that he was very big in the vegetarian and vegan world of culinary arts. But not a single picture. Despite the rule I had that only bad things come from Texas, I was curious that he was so off the grid being in the hospitality business. Was he ugly? Was he short or fat? Was he scared or did he have an eye patch? The possibilities were endless.

I gave a heavy sigh and then surprised myself when I said, "give me the information. And I will do my best to get Charlotte there. But like I said, Char does what she wants."

Max threw his hands in the air as if he was trying to kill a fly above his head. "Beggars can't be choosers right. I do hope to see both of you there. Oh, and wear that dress again. The one from last night. You looked hot as sin! Will could not stop talking about you. He also said you punched him. I guess mine was not the only eventful evening?"

"I didn't punch him! Well, I did but not like that. He grabbed me and I hit him. Well, he didn't grab me. He tried to get me to go to dinner with him and I refused and when I started walking away, he grabbed my wrist. Is he OK?"

"Yeah, he is fine. I think you bruised his ego more than his face. But he did say that you looked sexy as hell when you did it. And he would be replaying it again in the shower when he got home." He waggled his eyes at me and smiled a devilish grin.

"Get out of my store you ass-hat!" How dare he tell me what to wear? Who did he think he was? Despite my best efforts the corner of my lips lifted a little though at the thought. I hadn't been called hot in a long time. And I hated how much I didn't hate it. I would ask Charlotte if she wanted to go and even if she said no I would go. How could I not. If not just to taunt Max that he was not the gift to women, he claimed he was. I had to meet Dillon. I wanted to hear all about how he came to specialize in vegetarian food. The possibility of seeing Will had nothing to do with it.

Max left the paper with the number on the desk. I picked it up and thought about throwing it in the trash. If Charlotte went to the opening she could decide for herself if she wanted to give him her number but there were two numbers on the paper. Max's number and one other. I assumed that one belonged to the southern gentleman with a broken nose.

Chapter 9

Vionette

I loved Sundays. The bookstore was closed on Sundays so that meant I had the whole day to do anything I wanted. One of my favorite ways to practice self care was to go for a run in the park. I loved what running gave me. It was more than just the high. It was the escape. Running allowed me to think about all the things I wanted or it allowed me to not think at all. I started running after my parents' accident. I don't remember why. I am not a health conscious person by a long shot as evidenced by my fridge being filled with hot pockets and fast food leftovers. After my run in with Max yesterday I knew this is exactly what I needed.

After grabbing a croissant to reward myself for the exercise, I trudged up to my apartment. I had just sat down after a shower when my door swung open.

"It's just me! I have news and I had to tell you right away! I got you an interview at work. Apparently, the girl they hired was going through more coworkers than manuscripts. Anyway, it's

Tuesday at 3! It is happening, girl. YOU are finally gonna be an editor. Well you will be an intern for an editor but hey it's a start. And we can have lunch together each day! This is going to be amazing! Why are you not more excited? You look like I just told you your favorite book got put in a wood-chipper? Hello? Net? Are you there?" Charlotte waved her hands in front of my face. I knew I heard what she said but I was not able to process them. Can someone go into shock by hearing good news? I sat up on the couch and placed both feet on the floor and rested my hands on my knees, followed by my head. I tried to look excited but I felt like I was going to vomit.

"Wow. That is amazing Char. Thank you!" The words coming out of my mouth were not the words that were in my head. An interview? At the same publisher that I had wanted to work for in college. The one that I said no to because of the expectation that was placed on me. I had seen hiring ads now and then and had thought about applying but as soon as I went to fill out an application, Margie's face would come to mind and I would be overcome with guilt that I would even consider leaving the bookstore. She has done so much for me when she didn't have to that I owed it to her to stay. I felt like my heart would burst out of me.

Charlotte threw herself on the couch next to me. "I told them that you were perfect and even more qualified than I was to do the job. I am so happy for you. Now we just have to figure out what you should wear." I heard her as if she was in a bubble. It was my dream coming true but could I actually go? Luckily, I could decide that later. For now, I would enjoy the thought of it and work on not having a full panic attack.

Oblivious to my inner panic Charlotte asked, "What are your plans for this afternoon? I was thinking about going shopping, but I always want to go shopping. Wanna tag along? I know Sundays are your "me" days but I felt bad for ditching you the other night. Oh, I almost forgot! That guy that you punched last night. I think his name was Will? I ran into him at that sandwich shop near work. He asked me if I would give him your number. He said he needed to return your shirt? Exactly what happened between you two?"

Hearing Will's name somewhat stopped my heart from racing. I just blurted out the story as fast as the memories hit me. "It wasn't like that. Nothing happened. He invited me to eat dinner with him. I said no and when I turned he grabbed my wrist and so I punched him. He bled like crazy so I gave him the shirt I always pack for you to try and catch the blood."

Charlotte took on a predatory gaze. "We will come back to the fact that you keep an extra shirt for me. But did I hear you right? Did you say that you punched him for grabbing you? Was he trying to take advantage of you? Not that you getting laid would be the worst idea; I don't want it to happen by force."

That brought me totally back into focus. "No no it was nothing like that. Grabbed may be the wrong word. He reached and took hold of my wrist when I turned to leave. There was no ill intent at all. It just startled me. And I reacted. Unfortunately for him when I am dressed up and hungry and dumped by my best friend I get a little moody and so I hit him. I felt awful and tried to call or take him somewhere. He bled a lot but he said that was normal. That the nose bleeds really bad and it wasn't as bad as it seemed. He then said it wasn't the first time he had been punched nor the last but that he had never been punched by a girl in a dress like this."

I had never seen my best friend speechless but that is exactly what she was. I sat back down on the couch not even realizing I had stood up. "What did I do wrong? What is wrong? Say something please. You're freaking me out!"

She turned slowly to face me and she was smiling. Like a crazy psycho killer smile. "OK stop looking like that. That is freaking me out more than the silence."

"Nettie! YOU PUNCHED A GUY IN THE NOSE! Damn girl. I didn't know you were capable of such a thing. And why would you not go to dinner with him? He is hot. Like you cannot look directly at him, hot."

"First he wanted to take me to a bar-b-que place. Second he looked at me like I was the pig he was fixing to eat."

"Well, it has been quite a while since you were the main meal of a man!"

"And we both know why that is, don't we? Will is the exact reason I made the pact. Plus Max told me that he even said he would be thinking about me in that stupid dress while he was in the shower. The SHOWER Charlotte." I still could not believe he would say that after meeting me one time. Or that Max would actually tell me that he did. "I think we need to stay away from both of them and if they were not our ticket to the opening of the new restaurant then I would not speak to either of them again!"

"Wait, did you say that we are going to the opening of a restaurant?"

"Of course that is the only thing that you heard in all of that. Did you miss the part where I said that a guy was going to have special shower time while thinking about me?"

"I heard that yes and I have one thing to say to that. At some point you are going to have to come to terms with the fact that you are hot. You have that sexy librarian, shy nerdy girl thing going on. You make yourself untouchable. This then leads men to want to touch you. Honestly it's the reason the dare happened in the first place."

For the second time in this conversation my heart started to race. How could she bring that up? How could she think that about me? "Are you suggesting that what that bastard did to me was my fault?"

"No Net, that is not what I am saying at all. But I do think that the way that you are so closed off with the looks that you have does present as a type of challenge to some guys."

"Well, I'm sorry Char. Not all of us are so comfortable with being the town slut. Exactly how long did it take for you and Max to sleep together? One appetizer, two drinks? Did you make him wait through the entire meal and then, for payment, let him explore your many talents?" All I saw was red. I hated that I was saying these things, but I hated what she was insinuating more. So I stood my ground.

"I am more open and for your information we ate a lovely dinner and then dessert and then drinks and dancing. Max was a perfect gentleman. And yes I have my own issues with trust but at least I am experiencing something. Net, you're letting one thing stop you from having the one thing you have always wanted. I know you well enough to know that a stupid pact you made with yourself has not stopped the desire to find true love. I am begging you to forget Matthew and what he did. Live your life now. Put yourself out there. See what happens. You may get hurt, yes. But you could also find the love you have always wanted. Anything worth having is worth the risk of getting hurt. Even if it isn't with Will. You have to put the past in the past. Please. Now about this shirt that you carry around. If it's for me, it better be from a boutique! Only the best goes on this body! Men included." She gave her best sexy face and rubbed up and down her body. I could not help but laugh. And she had a point. I was letting him keep me from what I truly wanted. In trying to take control I was giving *him* all the power. Not anymore. I would start to claim myself again.

I walked to Charlotte and threw my arms around her waist. "Sorry I called you a slut. The shirt is from that little shop around the corner. And I will try and put myself out there." I meant every word. I did want to put the past behind me. But the funny thing is the past rarely stays in the past.

Chapter 10

Vionette

The best part of summer in New Orleans is walking around and smelling all the food. Restaurants will open their doors and windows to save on energy since it gets so hot. The sidewalks become mini sensory walks. It was truly magical for a girl who loved to eat. I was that girl. Surprisingly there were a lot of options for a vegetarian living in a meat society. While seafood reigned supreme on many menus, many establishments had a vegetarian or even vegan menu to choose from. And while Sundays were for me, my stomach made me realize that I needed food for her. Charlotte tried to convince me to go shopping with her but I told her that I needed time to process this new life I was going to try and live.

I replayed the fight with Charlotte and what I told her I would try to do when I walked into one of my favorite lunch spots. They had the best vegetarian muffaletta around. I opened my phone to look at what was happening in the city.

Then that voice came from my left.

"Good afternoon, Vionette."

It was like honey. I hated how my body responded to it. And more so, I hated that I didn't hate it at all. I turned to face him. Will was sitting in one of the booths facing the open window. He was dressed in what I assume was his version of casual wear, khaki shorts and a gray Cowboys t-shirt. His hair was covered by a Cowboys baseball hat. He looked like a frat boy. He looked like a player. He looked amazing. He was a little sweaty but that was normal for this time of the year. I once heard someone say that to know what it was like to live in Louisiana in the summer you should take a hot shower, immediately put your clothes on and then walk into a sauna.

"Hello, Will. I see your nose is healing nicely. Sorry about that again. Enjoy your meal." I turned back to order, and I heard his booth move. He was walking toward me. Why was he walking toward me? I gave him no indication that I wanted to continue the conversation with him. But here he was. Standing next to me.

Using his arms to brace himself, he leaned onto the counter top. My eyes automatically falling to his forearms. The girl behind the counter met his gaze and I think I heard her ovaries start to melt. I could not blame her. If I had not been wearing tight running shorts the evidence of my own melting would be running down my legs.

"Whatever the lady wants it's on me." He then looked at me and said, "I figured buying you a meal would be payment for taking the one you were trying to eat when we got booted out. And for making you feel as though you needed to punch me when I was simply trying to offer you company."

"You didn't make me feel like I needed to punch you in the

nose. It was a reaction. I panicked when you grabbed my wrist. And it was not your fault that we got kicked out of the restaurant. If someone should be buying someone a meal it should be me." I didn't want to buy him anything, but I could not keep meeting his kindness with rudeness. It was not fair to him or to me. Especially after the conversation I had just had with Charlotte.

Will could be the right person to try out some things. He was handsome and I was clearly attracted to him. He had been nothing but a gentleman in all the interactions that we had had. And he was probably not going to be in town much longer or at least not after the opening. Max had said that he was helping with the launch of the restaurant and that was taking place on Friday so then at most he would be here as a distraction for the next 5-6 days. My only experience with guys from Dallas was not a good one but that was not fair to assume all guys from Dallas were giant assholes. Will may just be the palate cleanser I needed. So, I took a deep breath. I stood a little closer and I placed my hand on his arm that was draped on the counter. "I promise I can buy my own food but thank you for the gesture. And I am still truly sorry for the nose punching and how I have treated you this far. Since you already have your meal I can offer some company. If you don't mind." I waited, holding my breath. Of all the things I had considered when deciding to play nice I hadn't thought of him rejecting me. At least not until I had already asked to join him. I searched his face for some kind of nonverbal cues that he heard me. What I saw was confusion. He looked down at my hand on his arm and then back up at me.

"Um…um…um…" Oh My God! I had rattled him. I had flustered him. "I would be honored if you would join me." OK.

First test down. I could do this.

"Thank you. I think it would be good if we just started over. Hello. I am Vionette Boudreaux. I am 24. I work at a bookstore that my aunt owns. I love to read, run and eat. I am a vegetarian. I haven't dated in over five years but I made a promise to my friend that I would start putting myself out there." Word vomit. That is what was spewing out of me. And I could not make it stop. Why the hell had I said all of that? Now I was going to scare him off before I even got the chance to practice.

He chuckled a little. Though he still seemed a little confused. "It's a pleasure Vionette. My name is Will. I am 27. I am in the food industry. I love to ride horses, find new and exciting foods and get punched by beautiful women in black dresses. I have dated a lot the last five years but nothing serious." His eyes lit up like a child on Christmas morning. His smile widened and I could not help but copy it.

"Nettie. My friends call me Nettie and I guess after spilling my life story I should consider you a friend. Plus, I cannot let you butcher my full name again. Is it the accent or are you just dumb?" I hoped he caught the flirtatiousness in the last part.

"Thank you, Nettie. The accents are so funny to me here."

"Our accent is funny to you. Now that is funny. Have you heard yourself talk? How-Dee Maim." I tried to evoke my best cowboy impersonation. Nailed it! " It's like you are straight from a John Wayne film. When we left the restaurant, I half expected you to have a horse tied to a parking meter." A genuine laugh escaped me. What is happening right now? I was having a good time. I was enjoying the banter between this cowboy and myself.

Will leaned over the table and I could not help but take a sharp breath and lean back. My brain said move away. Maybe he didn't notice. I am sure he didn't notice.

"I think if anyone should be flinching it's me."

Shit. "I wasn't flinching. They are bringing my food and I want to give her room to place it on the table." Just as I said it the girl dropped off my plate of food. Thanks universe!

"Right. I thought maybe you thought I was going to try and kiss you or something." He sat back, resting his arm on the back of the chair next to him. He was beautiful. Full lips. The kind that you would just melt into and …. No, I am not going to think about his lips. Crap. Now all I can think about is his lips.

"No. I didn't. I don't think that at all."

"Why not?"

"What?" I was placing the napkin in my lap when he asked the question. My gaze immediately shot to his and I remembered those eyes. One green and one brown. Both are waiting for an answer. All I could do was stare. I'm pretty sure I forgot English. My face turned red and my heart sounded like the track of the Kentucky Derby. Will leaned in closer again. He was no longer the aloof mystery cowboy in a restaurant. The left side of his mouth lifted slightly and he asked again.

"Why do you think I won't kiss you? Don't you think you're kissable?

No. "Yes. It's just that we are friends. And you seem like a nice guy and we don't know each other."

He laughed. I thought his voice was magical but his laugh. This man really was my own version of kryptonite. "I am not a nice guy. I am the kind of guy that sees a girl in a black dress and only thinks about kissing her. I am the kind of guy that asks around to find out where this girl likes to go and then visits each one hoping to find her there so that I can get her attention and get to know her better. I am the kind of guy that spends way to much time thinking of a night and wishing I had more game so that I could have gotten to know her better that evening. But it seems that my strategy paid off because I am here and you are here and judging by your face you have heard nothing I have just said."

Of course, the chase. Men never change no matter how much you want them too.

"I heard you just fine. I just don't understand it. You asked about me? After I punched you in the nose?"

"Darling, you can punch me anytime. And yes. I ran into your friend here and asked her for your number. She said something about sisters before misters. I explained that I had no ill intentions. That I only needed to return your shirt. She smiled at that and then told me that you come here on Sundays. And here I am and here you are."

I had to applaud Charlotte for not giving out my number. Especially knowing how much she wanted me to date. But she had told a complete stranger exactly where he could find me so we would be having the stranger danger conversation again.

"OK, so what, you just spent all day here waiting for me to come so you could ask me on a date? And just in case you didn't see me you had your partner ask me also? Forget nice or not. You're starting to fall into stalker status.

"First, if it meant being able to get to know you better then I would sit in a million cafes. Second, Max is my best friend not my partner. And third, I am not a nice guy in the sense of the kind you bring home to your mom. But I am the guy you should bring home to your bed."

Heat. All over my body. I could not look away. His eyes were almost glowing with sexual energy. And I don't know when it started but he was stroking my arm that was on the table in slow circles that did nothing but turn my brain to mush. The mental images that flooded my mind were no less tame than the burning sensation that trailed his fingers. It took my brain a minute but something he said triggered a memory. Best friend. He was Max's best friend. The best friend that has been at the restaurant all the time. Could it be? This man eating a plate of meat was Dillon Williams. Holy shit! Will was a nickname.

I mustered up the courage to ask, and I didn't know if I wanted to be right or wrong. "What is your full name? You have only ever called yourself Will. And I doubt you are famous enough to only have one name like Prince or Adele."

The circles stopped. He took a long breath in and leaned back into his chair.

"My friends call me Will. But the rest of the world knows me as Dillon Williams."

Chapter 11

Vionette

Oh my god! The man I had been trying to find any information on for the last two months was sitting across from me. He was drawing circles on my arm and flirting with me. And he was eating enough meat to feed a third world country. It's an interesting feeling when you build up a person in your mind and then you meet the real person and they are nothing like what you thought they would be. How can this be Dillon Williams? He was a vegetarian. He makes all this wonderful vegetarian food with the kind of passion that only a person living that lifestyle would have. But here he was and he was definitely not a vegetarian.

"How? You started all those amazing vegetarian restaurants and yet you're eating what I assume is half a cow."

"I am not a vegetarian. Never have been. I am a man who knows how to get what he wants. And when I graduated culinary school the vegetarian wave was starting. I saw an opportunity and ran with it. So I devoted my time to studying different ways to make vegetarian food interesting and delicious. And for a meat eater to do so says that anyone can do it. I made not eating meat seem attainable. I was working as a Sous Chef in a small restaurant. An investor noticed me and was looking to move into the restaurant business so we talked and he backed my first place in New York. We then opened one in Chicago and California. I thought of the idea of moving to New Orleans and I had hoped to do it on my own and buy our investor out but that didn't happen, at least not yet. I asked Max to come with me and he agreed and here we are."

"So why all the secretive life? I tried to find anything on you and not even a picture. Everyone under the age of 40 has some kind of social media. What's the deal with that, other than you are a serial killer or psycho. Which would fit your stalker vibe."

"I don't want to be the face of anything. I just want my food to speak for itself. And I mean as soon as people saw this face it would not be about the food anymore."

"True." Shit. Shit. Shit.

"So you do think I'm attractive?" He leaned back into the table and the circles started again.

"Will or should I call you Dillon? You and I both know you're attractive. The whole southern gentleman thing you got going on and all. Any girl or guy for that matter would swoon. I am just not that girl. I don't swoon anymore. I promised myself that I wouldn't. Not after what happened."

"What happened? And you don't have to tell me. But anyone that would dare make you not want to fall in love and be loved deserves the worst kind of torture. Point me to them and I will do it myself if only for ruining my chances to be that person."

I could actually feel the anger coming from him. He didn't know me. We were acquaintances at best and I believed with every fiber in me that he would hurt anyone that made a move to hurt me. "Oh and the name is Will. I told you my friends call me that and as you already said we are friends."

"Thanks Will. And what happened is not important. What is important is that I made a pact with myself that I would never put myself in a situation where I could be hurt like that again."

"But you must get lonely and it's a shame to have that body and not let someone worship it. You must at least miss sex?"

"You can't miss something you've never had." I said it under my breath. I don't know why I said that. I guess I really was comfortable with him. Those damn circles didn't help.

I had not noticed him take a drink of his tea until he spewed it all over the poor couple next to us. "What did you just say? And I am so sorry sir and ma'am. Please dessert. Anything you want. Two of anything you want." The couple looked at him still shocked and nodded in agreement.

"There went your too cool vibe." I laughed. A real laugh.

"It's not a vibe. I am cool. But no man would keep their cool when hearing that the woman of their dreams was also a virgin. How, and I mean this in the most respectful way, but how the fuck are you a virgin. You must have guys throw themselves at you all the time."

"Not until recently. And I guess I never met the right guy. I thought I did. We dated for a year. I made him wait and when I was finally ready I found out that I was just a dare to be conquered. He did not love me. He just wanted to get with me and then brag to his friends about how he slept with the nerdy girl with the big rack. After that I decided to swear off boys and focus on helping Aunt Margie."

I finished and noticed that something in his face had changed. He was acting weird all of a sudden. Like what I said had triggered a memory for him.

"Where is this guy now?" The anger was back. He was leaning all the way back and his hands were clasped together so tight I could see the white on his knuckles. His voice was no longer like smoke and whiskey but more like ice and steel. His jaws flexed and his hands were gripping the edge of the table so hard his knuckles were turning white.

"I am not sure. He was a senior. I was a freshman. He was from money so I always assumed he went back home to join the family business. His dad was a big tycoon in Dallas and likes to invest in startup businesses. I guess when I pictured Matthew Price I pictured him in a big office that daddy bought him with a wife and a girlfriend and a side piece."

Will took another big breath. He stood up and placed an arm on the table and one on the chair. Pinning me in. He leaned down and kissed my check. I froze and just let it happen. I could not think to move or speak or anything. When his lips left my cheek he paused and our noses could not have been more than an inch from each other. I looked into his eyes and they were even more impressive at this distance. "I have to do something so I will be out of town for a couple days. But here is my number." He gave me a napkin with his number on it. Then he gave me another napkin and asked for me to write mine. I did and slid over the piece of paper, one small move for woman kind but one giant leap for me.

"I think it would be best if we take this slow. I don't want either of us to do something thing that we would regret. Though I am sure there is nothing I could do with you that I would regret. There are several things that specifically come to mind." I could see his eyes heat with the words and had to fight the urge to ask him to describe them in detail.

He paused for a second and I thought he was looking at my lips.

"On second thought, fuck going slow." I didn'y have time to register what he said and his lips crashed into mine. I wanted to resist,but I couldn't. Before I knew it I was standing next to him with my arms around his neck and kissing him back. He devoured my mouth and slowly and gently used his tongue to ask permission. Which I gave without hesitation. And it was like swallowing fire. My entire body reacted. It wasn't just the kiss. Though this kiss was one for the history books for sure. It was him. I felt safe. Protected. Heard. And I didn't feel like a conquest or a challenge. In fact, this kiss made me feel like a prize. And I was actually wanting to play the game.

We finally broke apart. Both of us were breathing heavily. My eyes were still closed. He placed another small kiss on my lips. with incredible tenderness he held my jawline and traced my bottom lip with his thumb. "Thank you for telling me all that you did. And thank you for letting me kiss you. And thank you for not punching me in the nose."

For the second time I laughed. "You're welcome." It came out way more breathless than I wanted it to. I guess I lost my cool guy vibe now.

"You never said if you would be my date Friday?"

"Yes. I will."

His cheeks lifted with a smile and I could see the hint of a dimple in one.

"Until then."

"Until then."

He walked out of the restaurant and I watched him until I

could not see him anymore.

I heard a slight "hum hum." The lady next to me that was still covered in Will's spit take slid the chocolate cake to me with a smile and said, "I don't have a cigarette left but this should suffice. Don't let that one go. They don't make them like that anymore." He had chased and gotten the kiss. But I knew that this chase was far from over.

I knew she was right. I knew that I would be thinking of that kiss until I spoke to him again. I knew that I would be imagining what it would be like to have his lips on other parts of me. With a smile curling my lips, I felt the lady next to me give me a mental high five and for the third time today I laughed.

Chapter 12

Vionette

I had a date with a guy and an interview for the job of my dreams all happening in a week.

HA! How did this happen? I want to believe that I am ready for this. That I can put the past behind me and not care about expectations that have been placed on me by the one person in the whole world that cared for me when I needed it most. I could do that right? Just thinking those thoughts made me want to puke. So if I cannot pick them both I will have to pick one. Just as I was playing rock paper scissors with myself I felt my phone vibrate. I hadn't even made it a block from the sandwich shop yet. It was probably Charlotte asking to meet up or Aunt Margie asking me to come over for dinner. I did have a text, more like three from Charlotte asking when we would go shopping for the opening dresses and one from Aunt Margie indeed asking me to come to dinner tonight. But there was also one from another. And dammit if I didn't smile the second I read the name. As I was reading the text the phone started to ring. It was him.

"Just making sure you didn't give me a fake number."

"Glad to see that it is real and also that you're smiling looking at my text right now." He could see me. Of course he could, he hadn't been gone 5 min.

"Do you think I am the kind of girl that would give out a fake number? And I am smiling because my friend asked when we would go shopping for dresses for the opening. And as I am a girl I automatically smile when you mention shopping. It has nothing to do with you. By the way, you are not helping your stalker vibe. Safe Travels."

"It's not stalking if the girl likes it. And you clearly do. And you are so distracted that you're gonna run into a sign if you don't look up soon."

Just as I read the words and looked up I had to make a sharp turn left to miss a large caution sign.

"Now who lost their cool status. I will be leaving town tonight. But I wanted to let you know that I will be thinking about that kiss until I am able to give you another. I think my favorite place to think about it will be the shower with you in a certain black dress." I could hear the smile in the words.

He was good at this. Soon thoughts of what else he may be good at flooded my brain. Maybe I was out of my league. Will was clearly more experienced than I was. This may be too much. But my other option was to focus on the interview and that was not going to happen. So here we go. Operation flirt was in full swing.

"I think I may think about that kiss also. But I will reminisce in a much more ladylike place. Like the bookstore for example."

"Sexy. Don't get too crazy."

"Crazy is not in my vocabulary."
"Good to know. Till we speak again."
"Goodbye Will."

I hated how much my heart sank writing those words. I was starting to fall already. He kissed me one time. Two if you count the cheek, and I was envisioning all kinds of girly things.

* * *

I continued to think about those things all the way back home. I took a much needed shower, where Will never made an appearance. I decided to wear a long maxi dress to Aunt Margie's. She was old school and that meant no air conditioner. She liked to say that Mother Earth and Jesus would provide everything that she needed. To include a nice breeze. Unfortunately for her house guest, Mother Earth and Jesus rarely made house calls.

If Aunt Margie's store was a picture of the nineties, then her house was right out of the seventies. A ranch by every sense of the word, the house was bright blue on the outside. The inside was what I can only assume the color of pea soup that has gone bad would look like. The living room had orange carpet and her red leather furniture was arranged in two rows. It reminded me of a doctor's office on a bad sitcom. One wall had wood paneling and the chair in the corner was covered in orange and yellow and red sunburst. Honestly if you spun too fast you would feel like you were on LSD. But these walls had been my home for the last 7 years. And they were filled with just as much love and hope as they were brightness.

"Nettie, is that you?"

"Yes auntie, it's me. I hope you don't mind that I just walked in."

"No, not at all. I was just setting the table for our other guests."

"Other guests?" I turned the corner as I asked the question and I saw Charlotte on one side of the kitchen and Max on the other. Neither seemed to have known the other would be in attendance. But I didn't know they would be here either.

"Hey. Come sit down. We were just about to start. Maxi, you can sit across from Charlotte and Nettie Dear you can sit across from me."

I started to laugh a little when I looked at Charlotte's face. "Hey guys. How's it going?"

"How's it going Net? Really. Why is he here?" I didn't know that she had been practicing to be a ventriloquist as her lips never moved.

"He has a name. And he is here because a nice lady invited him here for a home cooked meal and good company. At least she was right on one of those things. No offense Nettie. I don't mean you." Max looked at Charlotte the whole time. There was malice in his voice but also something else I could not place.

"Hey Max. Good to see you too. How's the restaurant coming along? Will you be ready for the big opening? Oh and thanks for telling me that your friend Will was also your business partner and his real name is Dillon Williams."

I heard a gasp and Charlotte pounced on me. "No fucking way Net. Dillon Williams. The Dillon Williams you have tried to look up for the last several months."

Before I could get her to stop telling the best friend of the guy I had just accused of stalking me that I had done my own amount of stalking, Aunt Marge came back in the room with a large pot of gumbo. "Now I know that ladies have more rights than they did when I was your age and I am all for the empowerment of women but I will not have that kind of language in my house. Maxi is my guest and you will both treat him with the same respect you give me. Is that clear?"

"Yes auntie." I looked at the floor. I laughed a little at the fact that she was lecturing us on respecting her guest when she had just nicknamed him after a feminine product.

Charlotte looked directly at Margie and started to protest but was silenced with a look that only southern moms can pull off and joined me in the apology. Max grinned from ear to ear. I knew this was going to be an interesting meal as soon as Margie told us where to sit. I assumed she was working her bayou matchmaking on Charlotte and Max. As much as Aunt Margie wanted me to find love she wanted the same thing for Charlotte. "That girl needs to find a good boy to help settle her down." She would say it every time Charlotte came around or whenever I complained about the latest Charlotte escapade. I also wanted her to find love but I also knew what love could do. And so did she. But that is her story to tell not mine.

We all sat in our respective places. Uncomfortable silence filled the room. Each of us were angry at the other for some reason. Charlotte and I hadn't spoken since our fight and while we did leave on good terms it had been awkward. And I could only guess the tension between Max and Charlotte was because of the last night they were together. And I was furious that Max didn't give me Will's real name from the beginning.

"Well kids. This food isn't gonna eat itself. Dig in."

"It looks amazing, Mrs. Boudreaux. Thanks for the invite. I

had heard about southern hospitality but until now I had never experienced it." He glared at Charlotte with a hint of a smile. Brave man.

"I would think sleeping with a girl after a first date would be very 'hospitable.'" Charlotte glared right back.

"Charlotte, maybe not the best time to have this fight. Especially not in front of Aunt Margie." I felt embarrassed for her because I knew that Charlotte didn't get embarrassed.

"Oh it is. But usually a girl would like to stay and talk and get to know the person after, especially after she says it was the best sex of her life." Max clearly didn't get embarrassed either. Perfect for each other.

"I don't know about all that but what I do know is this is not the right conversation to have at the dinner table." Aunt Margie with the tie breaker. Hopefully we could enjoy the rest of the meal in silence.

"Charlotte, how is the publishing business going? I hope that you are finding books with something other than alien members."

Max spit his drink back into his glass. I couldn't help but laugh. Charlotte looked at Margie with wide eyes. "What do you know about alien members Margie?"

"I know that they are the only books that you young girls are reading. We cannot keep them on the shelf. No matter how I try to hide them."

"Well, the publishing world is good. in fact Nettie may be joining me at…" I kicked her under the table.

"Book club. There is a book club starting and Nettie may be joining me there." Charlotte looked at me when she said it but continued with the lie.

I knew I would have to tell her eventually but not now. And

certainly not in front of Max. Speaking of…

"Why did you not introduce Will with his name?"

Max looked at me and said, "I did. His name is Will. The only people he uses Dillon with are business people. You are not a business person so I used Will. Why don't you ask him why he didn't use his name?"

"I did. And he said his friends call him Will and he wanted to be friends."

Margie perked up. "Oh Net. Have you finally met a real life boy?"

"Yes. He is the head chef and partial owner of the new restaurant opening next door. We had an impromptu date earlier today because Charlotte gave him my schedule. And we are going to the opening on Friday together. It is not a big deal so can we not make it a big deal!" It was a huge deal. Not only for me as the self appointed hater of all things men, but that I had actually put myself out there. I am not an extrovert. I am not Charlotte who can make a man swoon with the bat of a fake eyelash. I am the nerdy friend in the corner that the guy goes up to to ask about the hot friend with the fake eyelashes. But today I was the girl the guy had asked about. I was the girl the guy flirted with. I was the girl who got the kiss. That was a huge freaking deal.

"When were you going to tell me? This is amazing. How did it happen. Give me all the details?" Charlotte was beaming with pride and joy. It was like what I imagine a mother's face would look like when her child takes her first steps. Proud and a little scared but mostly just love.

"I was planning to call you after dinner. But here we all are. And clearly, I am not the only one with a story to tell at the table. Why do I feel like you and Max are going to start a royal rumble at any minute? I told you mine now it's your turn." I glanced at Max who was stuffing his face and yet still managed a grin that would jump start any female libido that he unleashed it on.

"Yes Char…Do let everyone know what the problem is. I am sure that your friend's aunt would love to hear how hospitable her dinner guest has been to a lonely outsider." Max dragged the words as if they were lava coming from a volcano.

"Charlotte gave him the sweetest smile I think I had ever seen her give and said, "Fuck you!"

"Charlotte Piper. YOU will not talk to my guest that way in my home. Apologize right now." There was that drill sergeant voice again.

"Sorry Auntie. Sorry Max." She said the last part as if it was coming out like sandpaper.

"Now it doesn't matter what happened with you two. Water under the bridge and all that. I wont have your lover's quarrel ruin my good meal and company, ya hear! Now let's eat and if you cannot say something nice then don't say anything.

I sat there with my plate and ate in silence. What could you say after that? None of us wanted to rock the boat. And I could not help but think of the irony that I had had two dinners with a man opening a restaurant and both had been an absolute failure.

Chapter 13

Will

That Bastard. I was going to kill him. No, that would be too easy on him. I was going to rip him apart piece by piece. I could feel the old me coming back with a vengeance. My temper has always been my biggest weakness. From an early age I was strong and I discovered that when you are the strongest one on the playground you can have power. I liked power and control. So I used it. A lot. I got sent to kid jail the first time for breaking a kid's legs because he would not let me sit in my seat. The second time was when I sent a kid to the hospital because he was trying to kiss a girl that was clearly not interested. I never could see a woman being mistreated. Probably had something to do with seeing my mom treated like shit my whole life. But she put up with it because being married to my dad meant money and status. Two things I could care less about. I started counseling after the third time. I was paired with a firefighter captain. He taught me that power is never the issue but what we do with that power can be. So with his help I figured out how to tame the beast. And I also discovered a love for cooking. I would spend hours at the firehouse and my job was to cook. I loved being able to use my power for good. Cracking nuts and chopping things was a good outlet for my rage. And I was good at it. When I got my acceptance letter to the Culinary school it was the firehouse I wanted to tell. Not my parents.

But all the tricks that I had learned were gone and all I saw was red. How could he have done this? And to my girl. I knew he was a prick but I never thought he would stoop this low. I boarded the plane and prepared for the meeting, hearing Vionette's story played over and over in my head. I saw her sadness and her self-confidence be crushed. How could any man stoop that low? Not a man. A man would not do this. A boy would. A selfish, entitled boy hiding behind his fathers money. Money that was currently paying for half of my restaurant. But not after this weekend. I would find a way to pay. I would figure out how to get the money on my own. For her.

* * *

I walked into the bank. My head held high. My business plan under my arm.

"I'll let Mr. Jones know that you are here Mr. Williams. Can I get you anything? Coffee or water?"

"No thank you. I am good."

I had called the bank that handles my fathers estate on the plane and set up this meeting. I didn't like to use my name to make things happen but for her I would. I would do anything for her. Which was scary. We were not even dating. We had shared one meal at a diner and I was now rearranging the world.

While waiting my phone started to ring. I looked at the screen and saw the familiar name. I told him what I was doing as soon as I left the diner.

"Are you sure about this Will? This is a huge step. You have had one date with this girl and you stalked her for it. Just think about it for a minute." Max was saying all the things a best friend and business partner should say.

"I know. It's crazy but I cannot have his money pay for a single fork. He destroyed her. His son is the reason she doesn't think she is worth love. I have to get rid of all ties to him if I ever hope to move forward with her."

"I get that but just be reasonable. Don't put yourself in a bigger hole over a girl. And remember it's my name on the door also."

"I know. I won't do anything rash. I'll let you know when it's done. And if you want to walk away I understand completely."

"We made a deal bro. And I will be here when you get back. Besides, if I walk, who will bring in all the hot chicks?"

"Thanks Max. You are a great friend." I hung up the phone just as the large black door opened .

"Mr. Williams. Mr. Jones is ready for you."

I stood and made my way to the double doors. It was exactly how I would picture a well to do banking manager's office to look like. Everything was beige. There were no sentimental pictures on the walls or on the desk. No trinkets on the shelves. Just a monitor and a wireless keyboard on the desk.

"Hello Mr. Williams. I am Roger Jones. The branch manager.

I have handled your family's estate for quite some time. It is good to finally meet you. How can I be of service today?

"I need all of the money in my trust and I will need a loan for another $45,000 to be completed before the end of today."

I watched his eyes go wide for a split second and then he resumed the managerial stare. "I am so sorry to have wasted your time Mr. Williams but I do not think this is possible. The paperwork alone takes a few days and we don't do business on a Sunday. But I can get the paperwork started and can have everything finished by Wednesday at the latest."

"No. Today. I am leaving tomorrow and this needs to be completed before I return to New Orleans. I will pay whatever rush fees that I need to but it needs to happen today. Or I can start looking for other places for my parents to keep my money and perhaps put a bug in the ear of my parents also. I am sure they would not approve of the way that their only son is being treated.

"Of course, we don't want anything to give you a bad taste of our bank sir. I will see what I can do."

"Thank you very much."

* * *

After a few back and forth debates I walked out of the bank with the loan in tack. It was all mine. The restaurant was all mine. I called and fired my financier telling him that his money was no longer needed. He laughed and then I heard the email ping on his phone where I had bought his share out only moments before. It is strange when another person's lawyer likes you more than them.

I knew that this not only gave me the freedom that I wanted for my career but I could return to Nettie with a clean conscience. I could take her out on an actual date without seeing him in any part of us. I got to the hotel and thought about texting her right then but I decided to wait a little. After all I still had a few more papers to sign and I wanted to sit in what this meant not just for us but for me. I was free and I was in control. For once in my life, I could make the decisions alone. I was in charge of my own future. And I knew just what I wanted. I pulled out my phone and dialed.

Chapter 14

Vionette

That night when I got home something felt different. Something was missing or rather someone. I decided a bath would be just the trick to forget the horrible dinner with Charlotte and Max. So I gathered the salts and bubbles and my latest mafia romance and turned on the faucet. Just as I was sinking in, my phone started to buzz.

"Hello. You have reached the cool Vionette Boudreaux. She is unable to come to the phone right now as she is currently checking for stalkers. But please leave a message and she may call you back." I was pleased with myself. Cute , flirty and not at all over confident.

"Hello darling. How are you?"

I smiled. "I am good. How are you? How is business?"

"It's making progress but I would much rather be there with you. Charlotte dragging you to some crazy dance hall tonight?"

"No, I just left dinner with Margie and Charlotte and Max. It was tense to say the least so I decided I needed a stress reliever and it's been too long since I sat in the bath with a good book."

"Charlotte and Max together? I see the need for a stress reliever after what happened to them. But more importantly you said you were getting in the bathtub? Are you currently in said bathtub?"

I could hear the heat in his voice. Okay Net. This is your chance! Operation put yourself out there..

"I am."

"So that means you are not wearing anything?'"

"I am not. Well unless bubbles count which I guess they do as they cover up certain parts." Shit I was starting to ramble.

Lock it up Net. YOU can do this. He is, I don't know where, but he isn't here so relax! That was the reason for the bath in the first place.

"Bubbles definitely don't count. I must say I am having a HARD time believing you are not wearing anything right now, Darling."

"Well, how can I prove it?" I grinned as I said the words. My heart beat was rapidly becoming a distraction. Was this actually happening? I didn't have the experience he does. Does he expect a picture? Am I the girl to send a sext?

"They say a picture is worth a thousand words." There it is. I could see him grinning too. He was good at this but I am not that kind of girl. So I did what any good girl would do and I took a picture of my feet sticking out of the water.

There was silence on his end. I knew he was checking the picture but still. Why was it taking so long? Was that bad? That was bad. He is gonna think I'm a child.

"Beautiful,I have never understood the whole foot fetish thing but seeing yours I think I get it now. But it just proves you are in the water. Not that you are naked!"

"Well a good girl would never send a pic of her body to a stranger. And I am the very definition of a good girl. I guess you will just have to trust me."

"I am glad to hear that you are a good girl and I hope that you are getting the *relief* that you need."

I could not help but think of a different stress that needed to be relieved. I was thinking of his lips and his hands. He was waking desires in me that I hadn't felt in quite some time. Don't get me wrong, I am still human and when certain needs arise I know how to take matters into my own hands as it were. You cannot read mafia romance without feeling a certain type of way.

But since that kiss, all I could think was how he would be a welcome addition.

"Thank you. I am. When do you think you will be back in New Orleans? I am sure Max would like the help this close to opening." Atta girl. Deflect!

"I am hoping to be back on Tuesday. Do you have plans? I would love to take you on an actual planned date and not a stalker date as you put it."

"I will have to check my calendar and let you know."

"Okay. Sounds good. I promise no grabbing. Though there are several places on you I would love to grab."

"Really, such as …" Holy shit. This was happening. I didn't even mean to say it out loud. I just said what I was feeling.

Why is he not responding?

Did I scare him?

…

…

…

"You want to know where I would like to grab?" The words came out strained. Like he was holding back something in his voice.

"Yes. And maybe I could grab them for you since you cannot do it yourself?" Was I ready for this? Yes. No?

As if he was reading my inner thoughts I hear, "Nettie, are you sure? I like flirting but don't feel like you have to flirt back." He was giving me an out. HE was being a gentleman. And I wanted nothing to do with it.

"I don't feel like I have to. I want to. And besides you said to yourself that you are not a nice guy and you know how to get what you want?"

I heard him growl. He actually growled. I thought that only happened in vampire smut books.

"Darling, I am not a nice guy. But I am a respectful guy despite the fact that everything playing in my head are all the many ways I would fuck you respectfully disrespectfully. Starting with that mouth of yours."

Holy shit on a stick! "What else would you do if you were here?"

"First I would kiss you till you could not breathe without my breath coming out. Then I would trail kisses all over your body starting at your head and going all the way down to your toes. And where my lips left you would find my fingers softly caressing."

I could not help but trace the lines he spoke with my own fingers. It was hot. This was really hot and I was totally into it.

"Once I got to your feet I would make my way back to your center where I would no doubt find you ready for whatever 'nice' things I had planned. Like now. I am sure if I was there I would find you wet and willing."

"I am wet but I am sitting in water so that doesn't count!" Both of us knew that was total bullshit.

"Well then I guess the only logical thing would be to remove you from said water and then continue my exploration. Tell me, are you exploring yourself now?"

"Yes." My response was breathless and heated. My fingers had traced every path he said like a sinful road map.

"Once I removed you from the water, I would gently use my fingers to explore the most sensitive area at the apex of your thighs while also taking both of your nipples into my mouth. How am I doing Darling?"

"Don't stop!"

"Baby I won't. Not now and not ever. My fingers find that exact spot of nerves and using slow circles I bring you to the point of no return and just before that rush of pleasure I command your mouth to bend to mine. Vionette, are you using slow circles and being a good girl? Tell me you are?" He was just as breathless as I was.

I could not remember my own freaking name. I did exactly as he said. I continued the small circles he mentioned and as soon as his face with that dimple came to my mind I exploded. Pure pleasure cascading over my body. He had made me come faster and harder than I ever had with his voice! I could only imagine how my body would respond to him if these were his actual fingers.

"Vionette, are you still there?"

"I am here. I am great. That was an interesting story." What!!!! That was an interesting story. Are you serious? I will blame that one on the mind blowing orgasm I just had. Point to Will.

"Glad you liked it. I hope it helped with your stress relief." he chuckled lightly. Not pointing out that he clearly knew exactly how much it had helped.

"I can honestly say that I have never had relief like that."

"Well then it was my pleasure. And I am sincerely hoping I can show you my gratitude for indulging myself soon. I have to shower now. It appears that something here needs my attention. I guess you are not the only one needing some relief this evening."

I laughed out loud. "That must be so HARD for you. Too bad there isn't a girl in a black dress there to help you out."

"Oh there is. She is currently in a bathtub but she is right here with me in my thoughts. Goodbye Nettie."

"Good night Will."

I got out of the tub. My legs were weak and my brain was mush and my heart lighter than it had ever been. I was looking forward to Tuesday. I was looking forward to the next phone call. I was looking forward to my next mind blowing orgasm. And I was looking forward to it being with a man who actually liked me for me. I was looking forward to finally giving myself over to basic instincts and not second guessing the motivations for why Will wanted to be with me. I wanted to be with him. In every sense of the word. I was finally thinking about something more. I grabbed the closest pajamas and got in the bed. Hoping to dream of a chef in the shower!

Chapter 15

Vionette

When I woke up the morning after our phone call there were no less than 15 missed calls from Charlotte. I knew she wanted details of the date. I also knew that I wanted to know what happened with her and Max.

My alarm was still chiming the Monday blues and so I started my Monday morning routine. Wake up, shower, brush teeth. make coffee and then head to the store. I decided to wear my cut off jean shorts and a black razorback top. Messy bun and glasses complete my New Orleans summer ensemble. It was 112 degrees in the shade today and the humidity was 60 percent. If you want to have a good hair day then I suggest you don't live here. But I made it work. Did one more check in the mirror and walked out the door.

The whole city looked different. I knew that you could have a post 'O' glow but I had no idea that it would infect your whole vision. I wasn't complaining though. The city looked beautiful when looking at it through love. Wait? Love? Calm down girl. The man gave you one orgasm. Granted that was a good one. The best one. Maybe the only one I have ever had as my body has never felt that way before.

I made it to the store about 30 min before opening. I always gave myself extra time on Mondays just in case. And before I even made it to the door Charlotte grabbed me from behind. If it wasn't for her perfume I would have broken her nose too.

"What the hell Nat! I have been calling you since last night. I thought you were dead in a ditch or kidnapped by some creeper who was then gonna throw you in a ditch. I was picturing your news story. 'Here is the best friend of Vionette Boudreaux. Charlotte, can you please tell us what you are feeling right now in the wake of this tragedy?" Always the dramatics. She really should have been an actress.

"I'm sorry. After dinner I was wiped so I decided to take a long hot bath and finish my book. I lost track of time and then fell asleep with the ringer off. But as you can see I am not dead. Quite the opposite actually." I smiled. I tried to hold it in but I could not. "I am very good actually. The best I have been in a long time."

"Spill. Something happened after you got home. A bath doesn't give you that kind of smile but a…"

I smiled again. Lifting just the corners of my mouth and looking at her sideways. I am sure that I didn't need the blush I had put on that morning as I could feel my cheeks redden under her stare. I made my way to the door and tried to put my key in the lock when I felt a strong arm come around my shoulders and spin me around. She was not big but she was strong. Especially when she wanted information. Forget acting and the publisher. She should be a CIA interrogator.

"Oh. My. God. You slept with someone. Your face practically says 'I just got railed and loved it.' Who was it? I didn't even know you were seeing someone other than your fling with the hot chef. But I thought he was out of town for some mysterious business trip? So who was it?"

I knew that there is no way that I would be able to get out of this conversation without telling her something. But there was a part of me that wanted to keep it to myself. It felt like I finally had something that was just for me. And I didn't want to let it go yet, but I had to tell her something.

"Well it's not what you think. I did have a sort of fling with the chef but it was over the phone. It was incredible. I actually flirted and I think I might have been good at it. I mean he kept talking to me. And the man must have super powers because he made me come harder than I have ever been able to on my own. Like I am questioning if I have ever had the big 'O" before because of this man. And it was just with his voice. I may be in over my head."

Charlotte smiled and gave me a big bear hug. When we broke apart she was beaming. "Net. You like this guy. I am just happy that you are finally putting your heart back out there. Will seems like a nice guy and the sex is just the cherry on top. You know what I mean. Margie will be thrilled and it may even help soften the blow of your interview tomorrow. Have you picked an outfit yet? I think you should wear the black skirt and royal blue top that shows just enough neck and cleavage to show that you're stacked but covered enough to show that you are taken and off limits."

"I can always count on you Charlotte to make light of scary things. Thanks for being a good friend. The best actually. Truly. I don't know what I would do without you."

"Well your fashion would be terrible but you would make it. You're a strong woman, Net. You just have to find it in yourself again. And maybe Will can help with that. See ya later. Gotta get to work. Editors don't get their own coffee!"

She flitted out of the parking lot to her car. Charlotte was like spring after a long winter. She showed me how someone should be loved. I was grateful for her. She was the reason I had not been lonely these last five years. I was starting to wonder though if she would be able to fill the hole that would be left if something happened between me and Will for when he did leave. I knew even though we were not serious and this was all just a fling that when he left there would be a part of me that would miss him. She had done it once but would we be able to come up from the pits again?

As if on cue, my phone started buzzing and all the doubts left my head as a warmth spread over my entire body.

"Good morning, Darling. You look amazing. I think black is becoming my new favorite color."

Chapter 16

Vionette

"How do you know what color I am wearing? Are you stalking me again?"

"Turn around."

I took a deep breath and standing there five feet away from me was Will. He looked like sin on a cracker. Wearing dark blue jeans and a button down light blue shirt that was unbuttoned at the top. With brown shoes. He was the guy every girl described when describing their fantasy guy. And he was here. In front of me. Choosing me. I took a step toward him and then crossed my arms.

"I thought you were not a stalker. This seems pretty stalker to me. I mean you tell me that you are coming home Tuesday and then you just show up at my job unannounced. I'm starting to think you are a little obsessed with me."

His lips tipped at the corners and he took a step toward me. The electricity between us was intense. "Oh obsessed doesn't even come close to what I feel for you. After last night I knew that I needed to get back to you as soon as I could. And I didn't want to wait another day for the date that I promised." He walked toward me like how I would imagine a panther would stalk his prey. "So I sorted my business and then I got on the red eye flight back and here I am. I have actually been here a while. It seems you were very chatty with your friend." He was right in front of me now. I could smell his cologne. "And the conversation was so good I didn't want to interrupt."

I hit him on the arm. It was instinct. "You heard us talking. How much did you hear?"

His smile grew and his eyes heated. "Enough to know that you really enjoyed our phone call and that you think I have super powers."

I hit him again. I could feel my entire face heat for a completely different reason than it had a few moments ago.

"I don't think you have super powers. I think you have boundary issues. But I did enjoy the call. It helped take my mind off that horrible dinner and the decisions I have to make."

"What decisions? Is everything okay? He lightly took my arm and his mood went from predator to protector in a blink. And my heart melted for him even more.

"Everything is okay. Charlotte got me an amazing interview with the publishing company that I have wanted to work for since college. But I haven't told Aunt Margie and I am nervous because of all of her expectations. She took me in and raised me when my parents died. I owe her everything and I don't want to disappoint her. She is the only family that I have left." As I was talking, I could feel myself crawling into the weight of expectation. All of my butterflies that I had before had turned into bricks in my stomach. Just the thought of telling her was making me sick. What if I actually got the position and I had to tell her I would not be working at the store anymore. It was too much. It was too heavy. I wanted to feel good, not this.

I shook off the weight for now and focused on the fun in front of me. "I am a little shocked that I missed you." I looked back into those mesmerizing eyes and forgot all about what was making me anxious.

He grinned and said, "I missed you too but I am not shocked. Delightfully surprised maybe would be a better way to put it. I told you that I wanted to take you on a planned date. How's tonight sound? I was thinking about dinner at your place. That way you are in control. The whole time."

I saw a glimpse of something flicker in his gaze that looked like mischief. But I loved that he was thinking of me and letting me be in control of this. Knowing he was willing to go at my pace after telling him my sordid tale made me want him even more.

"I'll have to check my schedule. Us cool people are rarely free every night."

"Oh, I see. Well I look forward to hearing from you. Until then…"

His lips were on mine. But this wasn't the claiming kiss from the diner. This was more of a promise. He used his thumb and fingers to pull my face more toward him to give him better access. I melted into his touch. Never even thinking that it was 8:15 am and we were standing outside the store, basically in a parking lot.

We moved in tandem. I hooked my arms around his neck at the same time that he hooked his around my waist. His tongue gently coaxed my lips apart. When our tongues started their dance I became undone. I pressed harder into him, making promises of my own, I wanted to show him how much he affected me. I was not falling for his guy. I was having fun. It was a harmless flirtation and he was a nice guy that I was using to put myself back out there. I promised I would never give my heart away. But I said nothing about my body.

Somehow we broke the kiss and I had to remember how to think. Damn this guy could kiss.

"I hope to hear from you soon, Vionette. Have a good day."

"You too. See ya."

"Have a great day Mrs. Boudreaux. Hope you sell out of everything."

Shit. Aunt Margie had seen all of that based on the whistle I received upon entering the store.

"I knew it was hot today but good Lord. I didn't know it was that hot. Maybe I should start opening instead if that is what happens."

"Haha. Very funny. Good morning to you too. Now let's get to work. Those alien dicks wont sell themselves!" I smiled as I walked past her and I could feel her support and joy. She wanted me to be happy. She often said that it would fill her heart to see me take the store one day. And I was thinking of filling that kindness with heartbreak.

Chapter 17

Will

She could win any kissing contest she entered. This girl was my own personal brand of heroine. I could not get enough. I had finished that phone call and before I even hung up the phone I was looking for red eye flights back to her. She had woven some kind of voodoo on me and I was turning into more than a willing victim.

The second I saw her talking to her friend I lost my breath. How can one person hold so much power over another without even knowing it. Maybe that was what was so attractive about her. Don't get me wrong her body was incredible, but she walked through life not even having an once of a clue as to what she was.

My legs started moving before I even thought to tell them to do it. And I was kissing her before I registered her lips were on mine.

I tore myself from her. I physically had to make myself leave her or what I had planned for this evening was going to happen in this parking lot.

I made my way to the restaurant. Max was hard at work on making the finishing touches to the bar. He was covered in sawdust and paint. Earbuds in and singing way too loud to some Adele song. It was his favorite work music. He said her emotions really got him in the working spirit. In this moment, I realized that he was more than my best friend. He was my brother and as long as I had him I could do anything.

He spotted me standing in the doorway. He took out the ear pods and walked over to me. A goofy smile spreads across his face. "So are you officially my boss now."

"Sorry to have to say it but yea. Which means the slacking off stops now." He smiled even bigger and gave me a huge hug.

"I'm proud of ya my guy. You deserve it. What did he say when you told him? I would have paid good money to see his face."

"I let the email tell him and then I called and made sure he received it. He had no clue what I was doing or why. I thought about telling him that it was because his son was an absolute prick but I decided to let it go. He was still asking me questions when I hung up the phone."

"Savage bro. I like it. So how do you feel? All this is yours now." He did a turn and an arm move that Vanna White would be proud of.

"I feel amazing. I'm a little nervous, but I like it. I think I may even work a little harder knowing it's not only my name and my food but my own. Obviously you can be a partner if you want to. And it will only cost you $45,000."

I chuckled and so did Max before he said, "Too rich for me.

Besides, I am not ready to be a grown up yet. May never be. I like it right where I am. Handsome Sou Chef for my best friend in his restaurant that if it bombs has no ties to my checkbook!"

"Wow. Some friend you are."

"I'm the best friend. Speaking of best friends. Little miss spitfire next door is coming to the opening and she is bringing her friend. I don't know what is going on with her but I will win her over. No one says no to this." He waves his hands over his abs and chuckles. And I had to laugh with him.

"I know one girl that did and I am so very glad that she did. And yes. I called and talked to Vionette yesterday. She said she would try and get Charlotte to come but apparently there was some tension at dinner and she wasn't sure Charlotte wanted to see you."

"That's bullshit. I did nothing wrong. She is the one that just left right after sex. "

"Oh so she did to you what you have done to countless girls without a second thought. Poor thing." I chuckled again.

"I hate it when you make sense. We need to celebrate. Dancing and good food tonight? Two bachelors in the town."

"Can't. I have a date with Vionette. And I intend to do a thorough job of wiping that ass hat out of her mind."

"OOH. I like it when you show your dark side. You should definitely do that on your date."

"I don't think she could handle my dark side. But I'll keep it in mind."

I heard my phone buzz. I started to smile just reading the name.

"Oh man. You got it bad. When you smile over the text you're a dead man walking."

I threw a towel at him. I was smiling but I was not a dead

man. Parts of me were coming to life because of that name on the screen. Parts of me that had been dead for a very very long time.

94

Chapter 18

Vionette

The morning passed as it did most of the time. Numerous boxes were moved from one pile to another. No one was buying them so there was no restocking to be done other than the ones that I took home myself. I was beginning to wonder how Aunt Marge was keeping things going. I could not remember the last time that we had an actual customer. A big box store opened about 10 min away and with the draw of lower prices and gourmet coffee, even our usual hang out groups seemed to have moved on. Was this the universe telling me that I need to also? I loved Aunt Margie but soon she would have to consider what was more important. Her and my uncle had paid off the space before I was even born. But there was still a heavy overhead fee and the utilities had only increased due to the economy of the last few years.

As if reading my thoughts I heard a heavy sigh. "Nettie come in the office please. There is something I need to talk to you about." I took a deep breath and walked in. Much like her home the office was like traveling back in time. It even smelled old. But not like moth balls and old people, more like a cool basement at a friend's house. The kind that if walls could talk most of the people there would never find employment again.

"Are you sure I can be spared Aunt Margie? I mean the lunch rush is about to happen at any moment." I laughed proudly at the joke.

Aunt Margie smiled but it didn't reach her eyes. For the first time she looked, well, she looked old. "Dear girl. I don't know how to tell you this so I will just come right out and say it."

My heart sank to my toes. A wave of nausea like a tsunami hit me. Did she know that I had an interview tomorrow? How did she know? Charlotte. It had to be.

"This is just like her digging her nose into places that it doesn't belong. When did she tell you? It was after dinner that night wasn't it. She was mad at me and she told you about the interview so you would stop trying to play matchmaker to her and Max, right?" I was fuming. How could she have told her this knowing that I needed to find just the right time?

I could not bring myself to look at Aunt Margie. "What are you talking about? What interview?"

I didn't think it was possible but my heart sank even lower. "Charlotte didn't tell you about the interview that I have tomorrow with the publishing company around the corner? I thought that is what you wanted to talk about when you called me in here?" I was both scared and confused. If it wasn't the interview what was it?

"No dear. I have some news. I was talking with my financial planner and he is concerned about the future of the store. So I was thinking that maybe you could use your connections with your new friend and see if they would be interested in working together on something.

He wants us to become more trendy if we are going to keep the doors open. I have until the end of the week to give him a new business idea or he is going to recommend that I sell the place. So I told him that before I do anything I would have to consult my business partner and that is you. Now what is this about an interview?" She looked through me to my soul and I could not tell her about it then.

"It's nothing. Just Charlotte being herself." My heart was crushed. I had never been through an emotional roller coaster like this one. I knew that I wanted to make my aunt proud. I also knew that I wanted to be an editor. And clearly those two things could not happen at the same time.

"That sounds like a great idea Auntie. I have a date with him tonight. I can pitch it to him then." I would figure out what to do about the interview. That was tomorrow's problem. Tonight I had to get ready for a date.

"You have a date? My prayers have finally been answered. That is wonderful. I was starting to wonder if you were gay honestly. I was gonna ask and then I saw that kiss that you shared in the parking lot. Not that there would be anything wrong with that. I just want you to be happy. And he certainly looks like the kind of guy who knows how to make a girl happy!" She wiggled her eyebrows as she said the last sentence. And I would possibly never get that image out of my head.

I pulled out my phone and found the contact "not vegan chef" and typed the message.

Nettie: Turns out I had a cancellation so I am all yours tonight.

Thinking about wearing the black dress or maybe bubbles. What do you think?

...

Will: The black tank and shorts you were wearing today would be just fine. But if you were to greet me with only bubbles I would break a cardinal dinner rule.

...

Nettie:And what rule would that be?

...

Will: That you should never eat dessert before your meal.

...

Wear something comfortable. I will do the same. This isn't anything fancy.
Just two adults getting to know each other better over a good meal.

...

Nettie: Joggers and messy bun it is. See you at 6!

...

Will: Until then!

Chapter 19

Vionette

I had been on dates before. Granted it had been quite a while. There was the occasional boyfriend or 10 growing up. But nothing serious. I had my first kiss when I was 15 under the bleachers at a football game.

There was one time at a party my senior year of high school where I thought I might go all the way as they used to say. Me and Grant Jones were sitting on a bed at a house party. The make out session turned into his hand up my shirt and then him pushing me onto the bed. It wasn't that I didn't want to do it, it was more that I didn't want to do it with him or something like that.

I wanted my first time to be special. I know. Every single girl says that. But for those of us hopeless romantic readers, you want something worth telling as a part of your story. *"I was on a trip in Europe and I met a rich man who took me sight seeing and made love to me on the back of his yacht"* or *"I was a nanny and the cute grounds keeper would sneak me into the wine cellar at night and we would drink wine and make love under the stars."* Stuff like that. I did not want *"I was looking at a poster of Deadpool while a high school senior taught me that the anatomy class that we take did nothing to teach boys how to find the clit."*

Finally though I was ready to make that plunge tonight. I was only going to give my body. My heart was still locked away safe and sound behind the wall of concrete. But I was 24 now and I was tired of having the "V" card hanging over my head. Charlotte had suggested that I watch a few adult videos to get the just of things but after the first 5 min of the first one that I turned on I decided that going in blind was better. It could not be that difficult.

You can have all the confidence in the world when all someone sees of you is words on a screen. I had agonized over each and every text I sent him earlier. But I had 30 minutes to figure out how to get that confidence to manifest in the real world. I had spent the last few hours trying on every outfit in my closet.

I decided to wear something comfortable but also cute. Choosing my yellow sundress with giant daisies on it. It was not my cutest dress but it was the last dress that my mom and I bought together. It was my lucky dress. I had worn it for graduation from both high school and college. I was wearing it the day that I met Charlotte and the first day I started at the bookstore. It showed just enough skin to be seductive but not too much that I had to worry how I was sitting. It was loose and flowed off my waist but was form fitting at the top and did a pretty good job of showing off my boobs without being too much. I kept my hair in a messy bun. Since we would be cooking it made the most sense. And I actually liked the way that my neck looked with my hair up. I had toyed with the idea of getting a tattoo on my neck for that reason but when I pitched it to Aunt Marge she was less than supportive.

I decided on glasses since we were keeping it cozy and when I tried to put my contacts in, the dust from the store made sure that didn't happen. One last look in the mirror. I was ready for this. I liked Will and I trusted him. It was time. I would stop thinking about all the other stuff that I had in my head. And I would only focus on tonight. A girl finally becoming a woman. A woman going after what she wants. I finished the pep talk just in time to hear a knock at the door.

Chapter 20

Vionette

"Just a second." Play it cool Nettie. Make him wait a little. That was the right thing to do. Right? I took my time walking to the door. I removed the latch and turned the lock on the door knob.

When I pulled the door open I was not prepared. Will was standing there holding flowers and wine in one hand and a basket of groceries in the other. He was wearing faded jeans and a white button down shirt with the top three buttons open. His hair had that messy tossed look as if he had just rolled out of bed and it was hot as hell.

"Hello Darling. I hope you like red wine. I picked what would go with the steaks the best. And before you get worried they are portabella mushroom steaks. No meat at all."

"Thank you for remembering and red wine is perfect." I stepped to the side so that he could come into the apartment and it immediately felt small. He was a big guy and my apartment was definitely made for a smaller inhabitant. His presence filled the whole space instantly. As he walked by me, I could not help but glance at his butt. I had never looked at it before and it was perfect. This man was beautiful. I was used to being the second prettiest person in my apartment when Charlotte was here. I was not expecting that title to remain with Will.

"Are you there? Nettie?"

I came back to earth and he was staring at me as if he had just asked me a question. "Huh? Oh I'm sorry, what did you say?"

"Where is the kitchen? And also were you just checking me out?" He smirked a little.

"The kitchen is this way and what if I was? Is that a problem?"

"Not at all."

"Good. What are you making us tonight? That is a lot of groceries for two people." I watched as he started emptying the bags. He pulled out the steaks he mentioned, as well as organic green beans and potatoes. And a chocolate pie.

"I cannot bake so I picked this up at the bakery along with some chocolate mousse for the topping as dessert. I hope you like chocolate pie."

"I am a girl. It's the first rule of girlhood to like chocolate."

I walked over toward him. I had always thought that my apartment was a good size. But with Will here everything looked different.

The large kitchen was my favorite part of my apartment. It was a decent layout. There was a long window on the left side. The ample counter space was underneath the window and a few cabinets framed it nicely. I would open it in the fall and get a lovely breeze. Flowing in a U shape was more cabinets and the stove and microwave hood. In the middle of the room was a nice sized island with a farm sink in the middle. I always hated that the sink was on the island but it came with a cool function.

The previous owners had obviously had the same thought and had made a cover for the counter top that fit over the sink perfectly allowing it to become more space.

All in all a nice kitchen for a one bedroom apartment. I was looking at it through a whole new set of eyes today. Will took up most of the space.

"I am sorry about the kitchen. I don't cook much and by that I mean I don't cook at all. And by that I mean I can't cook. I am sure you are used to a much more professional set up." I looked at the floor. I was rambling again. He stopped unloading the groceries from the bags and smiled at me.

"The kitchen is perfect. And everyone can cook. You just need a good teacher and here I am. Where do you keep your pots and pans?" He looked around as if he could guess where they would be.

"Third cabinet from the stove on the bottom. But I don't have much." He bent over and looked in the cabinet and my eyes went straight back to his ass. It was a good ass. Tender and firm and just the right amount of...

"This is going to take me all night if you keep getting distracted by my butt. I asked you where your utensils were."

"They are in the draw above the cabinet with the pots and pans." My checks turned about 15 shades of red. I had been caught both times. Real smooth Net. My inner siren was laughing at me.

"OK girlie. Roll up your sleeves! Class is in session."

He had arranged everything in the prettiest and most organized way. I must have been zoning again.

"I don't have sleeves." I laughed a little knowing that he had looked me up and down when I opened the door and he knew full well that I was not wearing sleeves.

"I know. It is an expression or do they not have those in Louisiana? You said you cannot cook so I am going to teach you." His gaze met mine and I could not help but say, "Yes. That is fine. But I hope you have a number for take out when I ruin this nice food."

"I got it covered. Now wash your hands and we will get started."

I walked past him to stand in front of the sink. I placed the soap in my hands and started to scrub. He unbuttoned the two buttons at the cuffs of his shirt. He rolled one sleeve and then the other. I had never seen anything more attractive. His forearms were beautiful. Strong and manly.

He reached around me and grabbed the soap. How did he make the most mundane things look hot? I mean we were just washing our hands for God sake, but I could feel the tension just the same.

We finished washing our hands and started cooking. He was a good teacher which kind of surprised me. He was patient and did a good job of explaining things in a way that I could understand. We finished grabbing the last thing from the oven and the apartment smells incredible.

"Do you have a table or are we going TV dinner style on the couch." He was holding both plates and he looked even better than the food. "I don't have a real table but I do have chairs that go under the island. But I don't know if your lower half will fit under there."

"Have you been worried about my lower half for a long time

or just right now?"

"I am not worried about it. I just meant that you are so long, you may not fit."

"Oh so I am too big and long to fit in your island am I?" He smirked again but there was something else behind the smile. His eyes were like molten lava.

"No, I think you will fit just fine. I just want you to be comfortable."

"Oh I have no doubt that I will fit just fine and be more than comfortable." Then I heard it. Shit. Real smooth. I knew what he was thinking and that was not what I meant at all. How am I going to recover from this?

"It smells so good. I think we should dig in before it gets cold."

We ate and talked. I learned about his upbringing in Dallas and his parents. He came from money but he didn't flaunt it. He said he wanted to make a name for himself on his own. I respected that. Not that I come from money but after I moved here I became the bookstore girl or Margie's niece. Never just me.

We talked about our future goals. I decided this was a safe place and I could use Will to bounce off ideas about what to do about the interview.

"So did you always want to work in a bookstore?"

"Not exactly. I love to read and working there helps that hobby but my dream would be to find the next great American novel and help publish it. I want to find stories that haven't been told yet and make people read them."

"I don't know if you are aware but there is a publishing company right around the corner from the bookstore. You should apply."

"Funny you mentioned that. I have an interview tomorrow. Charlotte has worked there since Junior year of college. She got me the interview but I don't think I can go." I felt the wave of disappointment in me the second the words left my mouth. "Why would you not go? If that is your dream, go for it."

"Like you did with the restaurant? It's not that simple. Aunt Margie has always talked about giving me the store when she retires. She wants it to stay in the family. And so do I. She sacrificed so much to take me in when she did and I cannot break her heart. I won't. Besides, the bookstore does a good job." I knew that I was convincing myself more than him. I didn't want to disappoint Margie. Tonight was not about this though. Tonight was about other things.

And I needed to get the ball rolling on those things. I shifted my chair closer to Will and brushed my leg against his. "Tonight is not about figuring out the future. That meal was amazing. If any of that will be on the menu then I am sure the restaurant will be a huge success." His breath caught for a minute and his gaze traveled to where our legs touched.

" Yes well uh are you ready for dessert yet?" He got up as he was talking and before he could completely get up I placed my hand on his forearm and said "Let me get dessert. It's the least I can do after that meal. And besides, how hard is it to cut a pie?"

Surely it was not hard to cut the pie. But when I grabbed the knife to start I realized I had no clue what I was doing. He must have noticed cause I heard him coming up behind me. I started to just cut it like I would draw lines on a circle. I had two pieces ready for the plates. I remembered that I had smaller ones under the island. I opened the cabinet and squatted down to get the plates. I saw his shadow come behind me. When I went to stand up I felt my head crash into something hard but not as hard as the counter would have been. **Smooth Nettie.**

When I looked I saw his hand wrapped around the counter. His protective instinct went deeper than I thought. I walked over to the pie and started to place the pieces on the plates. I could feel him behind me. He was not touching me but there could not have been room for more than a secret. I could feel his heat and my own body temperature started to rise. I could not see what he was doing behind me but I was hyper aware of his front touching my back now.

"Why did you want to make sure that I had control of this night?" Direct was the best way to deal with this right. I was an adult and so was he.

"I know that you have been hurt. I also know that you are a virgin. And while that doesn't mean that you are inexperienced, it means that I have to be careful with you. I don't want to push too hard or go to fast. No matter how much the phone call and that kiss this morning made we want to say fuck it to both of those things."

"Does my lack of experience change your opinion of me? And just so you know your experience doesn't make a difference for me. I am sure that with those looks you have had your fair share of women throw themselves at you."

"None that mattered," He whispered in my ear and he reached for the chocolate mousse. Taking his finger he gently dipped it into the chocolate and instead of placing it in his mouth, I felt his finger trace over my shoulder. I shivered and my legs grew weak. Before I could collect my thoughts he dipped his head to my shoulder and I felt his tongue tracing the same line that his finger had moments before.

"What are you doing?" My eyes were closed. My words were

breathless and my center was already soaking.

"That is for the pie sir."

"I know. But as a chef I have to try new and exciting ways of presenting the food to make it more appetizing. And the shoulder of a beautiful woman seemed like a good idea." He placed his finger in his mouth and licked the rest of the cream off. Visions of other places I wanted his mouth came to my mind.

The corner of his mouth hitched up just a bit and he said "I was right. Tasted way better than it will on that pie."

"Okay but now I am all sticky. And it's your fault." I was holding onto the counter top so that I did not fall. My legs were traitors and I had never been more appreciative of underwear than I was right now. If not for them I am sure we would be standing in a puddle.

He laughed. He then reached around to the other side of me and grabbed a paper towel. He turned on the water and wet the paper. Trapped between his arms, my breath caught. What the hell was he gonna do with that? He wrung out the water and wiped my shoulder teasing the same line again.

"There. Not sticky anymore." He was starting to get a little breathless also.

"Well I'm not sticky but I am all wet." Completely drenched would be more accurate. I started to turn to face him but he stopped me, trapping me again between his two arms.

"If you turn around right now then two things are going to happen. First I will kiss you until you can no longer remember your name. And the second is we will have wasted this pie that you so expertly cut because I will have you as my dessert right here on this island."

I saw his forearms flex and the promise in his voice. No

longer playful and light. He was dominant and hot. Now is the time. If I was going to back out now would be the time to do it. Was I ready for this? I looked to my right and left at his arms. His fingers were still wet from the sample of chocolate mouse he had.

Yes. Yes I was!

"What if I told you that I don't really like pie anyway?" I completed the turn and looked him right in the face. "In fact, I would say that right now there is only one thing that I am wanting and it has nothing to do with food!"

Chapter 21

Vionette

I had just gotten the words out when his lips crashed onto mine. It was not careful or slow. It was a passion. It was want. It was hunger. He pulled me to him and lifted me onto the counter. I instinctively wrapped my legs around his waist to limit the amount of space between us. We were devouring each other. His breath was my breath and it was like I was breathing for the first time. Why had I made the pact. I had been missing this and it hit me then just how lonely I had been. He broke our kiss and looked me in the eyes and said, "Nettie. I have thought about this ever since you punched me. And imagined all the different ways that I wanted to show you how you make me feel. But I need you to say that you agree to it. I will be tender the first time. Is this really what you want?"

"Yes. 1000 times yes."

And with that he stopped holding back. He deepened the kiss. He placed my hands on his shoulders and held my chin between his finger and thumb. He traced my lower lip with his thumb.

"I have wanted to taste these lips again since the deli. If anything becomes too much you just tell me to stop okay. You are in control."

"Okay. I will."

"Good girl." The left corner of his lips lifted for a fraction of a second and then he kissed me again and grabbed my bottom lip with his teeth. The sensation flew right to my center.

"Delicious." He moved his hands to my throat. "I have also imagined what it would be like to grab this beautiful neck and squeeze, making the sweetest noises come from your mouth and feeling the vibrations that those moans make."

"Yes. please."

He moved his hand to my throat and he placed his thumb on one side and the other fingers on the other. Using just a little pressure he squeezed and just like he said a moan came out of me. "That feels amazing but I want more." I said it without hesitation.

"Patience Darling. I said I was going to be gentle the first time."

I wanted his hands on me. I wanted him to touch everywhere all at once. I wanted him to claim me the way the men in my books claim women.

He moved his hands lower and started to cup my breast. I looked down where his hands were holding me and marveled at the way he looked. I could see the strain on him that going slow was taking. I could also see that another thing was straining further down.

"Eyes on me Darling. I want to see you experience this. I want to see all of you. Which would be much easier if this beautiful dress was not in the way."

"Then take it off." I almost screamed at him.

"Yes ma'am." He chuckled and picked me up, lifted the hem of my dress and placed me back on the counter. I lifted my arms and the dress was discarded on the floor. He took a step back and looked me over.

"Beautiful."

I waited for the urge to cover myself. It didn't come.

He stepped toward me again and kissed me. He cupped both breasts and trailed kisses along my neck. Breathless I melted into him once more.

"Which way is your bedroom? While I want to make good on the promise I made earlier, I don't think the first time that I tasted you should be on a cold counter top."

"Down the hall, last door on the left."

I said the directions and then I was in the air. I wrapped my legs around him once and I could feel his erection hit my center and a wave of heat washed over me. He opened the door without ever breaking the kiss. I felt the edge of the bed on the back of my thighs and then I was sitting on the bed.

"I am going to take off my shirt. Then I am going to take off my pants. Afterwards, I am going to remove your underwear. I am going to kiss every inch of you and then I am going to make you come on my tongue."

"That sounds like a good plan."

"Thank Fuck for that. I may have died right here if you had said no."

He started to unbutton his shirt and then his pants and he was standing in front of me in only boxer briefs. He was spectacular. Like a statue coming to life. Not perfect by any means but perfect for me. I could not help but to say "You're kind of beautiful, Sir."

"Thanks but it's not me I am worried about right now." He knelt down between my knees and grabbed the sides of my underwear. He looked up at me silently asking for my help with the last part. I lifted my hips just enough so that the underwear could slide off easily. I was trembling. Either of anticipation or anxiety, I was not sure.

"Why are you shaking? Is this too much? Just say the words and I will stop. Remember you are in control."

"No, don't stop. Ever since that kiss in the diner I have wanted this. I want this with you. I am just nervous. I may be bad at it."

"That is not possible." Once again he was over me kissing me. Both his hands on either side of my head. His body pinning me to the bed. I didn't feel trapped though. I felt wanted. I felt desirable. I felt beautiful.

He broke our kiss and met my eyes. "I am going to kiss your neck and then your breast and then your stomach and then I am going to make my way to your center. I have wondered what you taste like here also." As he said it I felt the softest touch graze over me and it sent a new shiver down my body.

"I love how responsive you are to my touch. You are doing such a good job Darling."

He started kissing my neck. And quickly moved to my breast. He was so gentle but I could tell he was holding back. His face was marble. But his eyes were pure lust. I was responsive to him but he was clearly responding to me too.

He made his way lower to my stomach. When I felt his lips near the line my underwear would be, I breathed in sharply. "Are you okay?"

"Yes. I am just nervous. Maybe it would help if I could watch somehow. So I know what you are doing? Is that possible."

"You want to watch me fuck you? Is that what you are asking?"

"Yes. Is that wrong?"

"Jesus Christ Net. How are you even real? No there is nothing wrong with that at all. Turn this way."

He had apparently noticed that my bedroom had a full length mirror hanging from one of the closet doors. He turned me so that I was now seeing my entire reflection in said mirror. And looking at myself with this god of a man standing in front of me I could not help but think that I look hot.

He moved behind me and grabbed my face while using his other hand to caress my breast. "Look at yourself, Net. See how you respond to my touch and how you make me respond. Keep your eyes on yourself the whole time. No matter what, okay?"

"O-okay."

He didn't go slow this time. He went straight back to the same position. On his knees between my legs. This must be what power feels like. I understood the draw of this for women now. I felt sexy and powerful and desirable.

Just as I got used to the feeling a whole new feeling took its place. Pleasure. He kissed the inside of my thigh and then the other and then he devoured me. His tongue was magic. Using broad strokes he licked the very center of me. I tried to continue to watch but my eyes closed and my back arched on instinct.

"Keep watching."

I forced myself to look back at the reflection and no sooner had I made eye contact with myself did the biggest wave of pleasure hit me and wash over my body. Before I could stop it

I let out a moan but it came out more like a scream. He was on his feet and at my side in a heartbeat.

"I'm okay, that was incredible."

"I am glad. But I have way more to offer. Lay back down. I am going to do the same thing but with my fingers inside you. It may hurt at first but I promise I will be gentle.

"Yes. Please."

"Lay back down. But keep your eyes on mine this time. And don't look away no matter what. Can you do that?"

"I think so."

"Good girl."

He took his position between my legs once again and then looked at me. "I am going to lick you from top to bottom and then you will feel a slight pressure and then nothing but pleasure from then on. I promise."

"Okay. I trust you Will."

Both of us were panting. His patience was incredible. True to his word, I felt the familiar heat and wetness of his tongue. Then I felt the first pinch of pressure. And slowly he let his fingers sink into my core. It did hurt at first but just as he said the pain gave way to the most amazing pleasure. Looking at him while he worshiped my body brought another word to my mind; careful. He was being so careful. With my feelings and with my body. And I wanted to repay that with something but what did I have to give but more of myself.

"Will, Stop."

He immediately stopped and a look of concern took over his once lust filled face. "Are you okay? Did I hurt you?"

"No. Nothing like that. This has been incredible. But it feels a little one sided."

"Christ Nettie. Can't you see that this is giving me all the pleasure right now. Hearing your moans and knowing they are mine is incredibly hot and I am having to use all of my willpower to not take you hard and rough."

"Why do you not want to go hard and rough?"

"Because it's your first time, Darling. You have to learn to walk before you can run." His eyes held mischief in them.

"I am pretty fond of running though." I met his gaze and hoped that he would be open to what I was asking. I didn't want him to see me as the virgin girl he had to protect. I wanted to be his undoing in every way.

"What do you want then darling? You're in control after all."

"Well it seems only fair that you got to taste me so I want to do the same."

I could feel him tense as he held me. He sucked in a slow breath.

"Granted I may be bad at it so you will have to tell me what you like. I mean I think I have the basic concept but I assume, like us gals, every man has what he likes right."

He cupped my face in his hands. And kissed me softly on my lips. "You are perfect Vionette. I want to make this experience one that you will always remember so if that is what you want then that is what you will have." He stood in front of me and started to remove his boxers. My mouth went dry. My eyes went wide and I could not stop the gasp that escaped my lips. He was massive. And while I probably should have been scared I was drawn to him.

I didn't think. I just let nature do the leading. I knelt in front of him and replaced my hand with his. I had some idea of what to do. I had given hand jobs before and I had seen adult movies. As soon as my hand grasped him he moaned. And his head tilted back.

"Fuck Nettie."

Taking a play out of his playbook I said, "I am going to use my hand first and then I will take you in my mouth. You can use my hair to guide me to what you like. Is that okay?"

"Fuck. Yes. Please."

I started stroking him, up and down, in slow smooth strokes.

"How can such innocent hands be so dangerous? I am hard as stone. See the way that you affect me."

I smiled. I looked back up to his face and as soon as our eyes met I took him in my mouth. I was pleasantly surprised by the taste of him.

"Shit baby. That feels so good. If you keep that up I won't last long and I want the first time you make me come to be inside you. I want us to come together."

I continued to suck him. Stopping to lick up the underside of his dick and then placing him back in my mouth. He wrapped his fingers in my hair and told me the pace that he wanted. I tried to take him more fully in my mouth but I gagged.

"Remember Walk first." His words were strained and I could barely hear them.

He finally lifted me with my hair. "If you continue that neither of us will get what we want. And all I want right now is for my cock to feel you from the inside. Lay down on the bed."

I didn't question him. This whole thing was about building trust and I trusted him completely. With my body and my soul. I laid on the bed and looked up at him.

"I am going to kiss you Nettie. And it will not be a gentle kiss. Once you are relaxed into me then I will slowly start to fuck you. I will try to be gentle but I may not be able to stop myself. If it gets too much just say stop and I will. But you may have to scream it. If your pussy is half as good as your mouth I will never want to leave. Are you ready?"

"You have no idea how ready I am."

He kissed me with all the fire that he had been holding back. He devoured my every moan and noise. And just as I was getting impatient I felt him at my entrance.

"Yes Will. I want this and I want you. I don't want to walk. I want to run as long as you are running with me."

And that was that. He impaled me with one broad stroke. I gasped and screamed a little but not a 'holy shit that hurt' scream but more of a 'holy shit that feels amazing' scream. He broke our kiss and sat up. We made what I would think a drunk 'L' would look like.

"Raise up on your elbows Nettie. Watch us join together. We fit so perfectly. You feel like heaven and hell at the same time. My deepest desires and my wildest dreams."

I lifted like he said and looked down. He was pumping in and out and filling me so completely. Every stroke hitting just the right spot. As the pleasure built I could feel his hold on my legs tighten.

"You're doing such a good job baby and I don't think I can hold back anymore. I need you to come. I want to feel you squeeze me. I want us to come together and never come back down. Can you do that? Come for me Nettie."I could not tell if it was his words or the peak of my pleasure or both, but I erupted. I could feel my muscles squeezing him. I moaned and called his name. He continued his stroking and then I heard him moan with his release. We collapsed on the bed together. Both breathless and covered in sweat.

I opened my eyes and I saw the most beautiful eyes staring back at me. I never expected to find a man like him. I had grown up with tales of knights in shining armor. My own town was the setting of a movie about a girl kissing a frog that turns into a prince. Until now, guys I had kissed turned to rats. Never princes. Until Will.

"Well, I guess it's true. A man that is good in the kitchen is good in the bedroom!"

His eyes sparkling with desire once again, "I am glad you enjoyed yourself."

I didn't want to be that girl but I could not help the question come out of my mouth.

"Did you? I mean did you enjoy yourself? I'm shit in the kitchen as you learned today and I have very limited experience and…"

"Shut up." His lips pressed hard against mine and I was melting into him all over again.

Chapter 22

Vionette

When my alarm sounded the next morning, I had a horrible thought that last night was just a dream. I rolled over and the bed was empty. Was it a dream?

That didn't explain why everything in this house smelled like him. Or why I was so beautifully sore. But there was no one in the bed with me. Had he just left. Will didn't seem like the kind to do that. But then again what did I actually know about him? We had only had one dinner and I spent most of the time talking about myself.

I covered my head and started counting all the ways that I was naive and then I heard the slightest cough.

"I am fully prepared to spend the entire day here in this bed with you but you need to at least try and eat something."

My heart soared. I smiled into the pillow. Play it cool. Calm down. It wasn't a dream. It was real. I lifted the cover and turned. The face in the doorway was spectacular. His hair was disheveled but suited him. He was only in his underwear and as far as I was concerned he should never wear clothes again. He was holding a tray of something that smelled heavenly. My stomach reacted and let out a loud gurgle.

"I guess my stomach agrees. That smells amazing."

"You were amazing. You are amazing."

"You were pretty good yourself." I smiled a little as he set the tray over my lap and lightly kissed my check.

"Are you sore? I can run a warm bath?"

"A little but I am okay. Thank you for last night. It was incredible."

"I think that I am supposed to say thank you to you."

"I hope that you enjoyed yourself as much as I did. I mean really did. Really really did. I knew that sex could be good but holy shit. I had no idea. If I had known I would have done that much sooner."

Shut up Net.

He laughed and it was deep and rough and hit me right in the heart. I could not figure out the feeling that I had. It was beyond satisfying. It wasn't comfortable. It was more than that too.

Then it hit me.

Safe.

I felt safe. How could I feel safe with this man? For one he was a stranger in so many ways. We had only had one real date and yes we talked about things but the talk was more of a dance to relieve the awkward tension. We both knew what would happen last night. And I had made that decision with little to no thoughts about how the next day would be. Did I want to be more? Did I want this to continue? The answer to the last question I knew before I even got the whole question out of my mouth.

Before I could dive any deeper into the thoughts of a non virgin, I heard him ask me something. I hadn't even realized that I was staring at him. "Huh. I am sorry. What did you say?"

"I said what time is your interview today? Or did you decide not to go through with it?"

And with one question my bubble popped. I was blissfully happy and floating and then I came crashing to Earth again. I had totally forgotten that it was today. Not only today but in just a few hours.

"It's at 3. And yes I think I am going to go through with it. But I still don't have a clue how I am going to tell Aunt Margie. She wanted me to ask you for ways that the bookstore and the restaurant could work together to bring in more people. How am I going to tell her that I don't want to ask you that question because I don't want to work for her anymore? It will crush her. And she has been so amazing! I cannot break her heart. She was the only one other than Charlotte who helped me put mine back together."

"I understand that you love your aunt. And as someone who is less than satisfied with my family, I understand that you don't want to disappoint her. But I have seen how much your aunt loves you Nettie. She will be so proud of you for chasing your dreams and even more proud of attaining them." He gently puts the hair falling in my face behind my ear. He cups my face in his hands and I cannot help but notice how perfectly they fit around me. I smile at him and take a deep breath and then remember that he brought food. "What smells so good?"

"I wasn't sure how you liked your eggs so I made them three ways. One is my favorite and then two more that we offer at the restaurant. And then some french toast with extra powdered sugar. You seemed like a sweet girl more than a savory."

"I think I am beginning to like the savory also." I let my eyes roam freely over his frame. I started to feel a hunger growing deep within me and it had nothing to do with the eggs. I sat up onto my knees and moved the tray of deliciousness out of the way. I straddled his lap and placed my arms on each of his shoulders clasping them behind his head. I leaned into him until our noses were an inch apart and then rested my forehead on his. "Thank you for the eggs. Thank you for last night. And thank you for the pep talk."

"You are more than welcome." He lightly placed a kiss on the corner of my mouth. "I am more of a savory man but I think I am beginning to like sweets!" I returned the kiss and continued it until we were both breathless.

"Don't you have work to do? Wouldn't want to be late to the job you do have. Just in case." He winked at me and pulled away from the tangle that our bodies had become. I instantly felt empty and fought the urge to grab him and keep him right where he was.

"Yes I do."

After the make-out session and the eggs, which is my new favorite food, I said goodbye to Will. I had to get ready. Ready for work. Ready for the interview and ready to crush the dreams of the greatest person in the whole world. I used the shower to both practice my interview skills but also to write the speech in my head of what I would say to Aunt Margie.

"Well, I think I am qualified for this position because I have a degree in English lit and marketing. With a minor in communications."

"I know that you want me to take over but I don't think I can do the store justice. I am not good with people."

"I see myself as a full time editor in 2 years with an eye for new voices that bring strong female characters to the forefront of fiction."

"I have no idea where I see myself in 2 years, Auntie. I am 24. I am still trying to figure out what I am going to be doing tomorrow."

This was going to be a disaster. I finished my shower and decided to wear my normal work clothes and then change before the interview at the cafe down the street. As I was drying my hair, a process that is basically futile living in Louisiana in the summertime, my phone screen lit up. I picked up the phone and unlocked the screen.

My heart sank to the floor. A wave of nausea rolled over me like I have never felt and I was both hot and cold at the same time.

It was him. Matthew. Why was he messaging me? And today of all days. I was already rattled enough, but I guess the universe thought I needed to be even more on edge. I just stared at the screen. Then the dreaded typing bubble showed at the bottom of the message. He was typing again. I had not even read the first one. I had not made it past the realization that he was texting me in the first place.

"Vionette. Hey. It's been a long time. I hope you are well. I will be in town for a few days for some friends and I was hoping that I could see you. We need to talk about that night."

*****

"I can meet you at the cafe that you stop at after you run. Do you still run? I am sure that you do. Anyway I will be there Thursday at 4. I really hope to see you there."

Was he fucking serious? Did he really think that I would meet him? How could he want to talk to me? How could he think that I would want to talk to him? I was going to stop this now before he got his hopes up.

"Matthew. It has been a long time. But not long enough. I do not want to talk to you about that night or any other. Enjoy your trip but go to Hell!"

Precise. Unfeeling and just the right kind of mean. I was proud of that response. What could he possibly tell me that would be worth my time. Surely he didn't think that I cared about what was happening in his life. I had hoped he would have been hit by a bus. Or maybe been the victim of a work deal gone wrong and ended in a mafia sniper taking him out once and for all. Apparently none of those had come true.

I had bigger things to deal with today. I put on my favorite cut off shorts and a red tank top. I placed my hair in a braid and grabbed my bag with my interview clothes in them as well as my resume. As I walk out the door, I think about the message. And I cannot help the curiosity that comes with it. Maybe meeting him would not be so bad. After all, I had punched one guy this month. Might as well add another to the list!

Chapter 23

Will

INCREDIBLE.

That was the only word to describe the last 19 hours. I had started the day with my girl in a parking lot. My Girl. I liked the sound of that. I had formed ideas in my head about how our first time would be long before I knew she was a virgin. I mean a guy would have to be dead to look at a girl like Net and not think about sleeping with her.

I also knew, after our cafe date, that she had been hurt by someone she cared about deeply. And worse, I knew him. I went to school with him. I was his friend. Well we were all friends. We met over the summer. His dad was a financier and got me and max our first internship which led to getting into culinary school. My parents were friends with his parents and we would often see each other at the same vacation homes. We would run wild and free as all twenty year old boys do.

It was the second summer that Mathew told us he was going

to school in New Orleans for a bit. He got into a business program there and he wanted to see if he could make it without his dads help. Granted his dad had helped him every step of the way.

So we went our separate ways. A few summers passed and Max and I graduated culinary school and set out for New York. Matthew also made his way through business school and ventured to New York to help run his fathers businesses there. We reconnected when his father decided to give us the money to open our first place. Matthew was at every opening we had. Drinking and laughing and saluting our success. He was a good friend and it was as if no time had passed and we were those same 2o year old boys.

One particular evening, we found ourselves in a bar. The whiskey poured and the words flowed. Max about his many conquests but none that challenged him like he wanted. Me being the only gentleman and not kissing and telling. And then Matthew told us this tall tale of a smoking hot freshman he had met his senior year. He had talked about how he had seen her and tried to talk to her but she wanted nothing to do with him. And not being one to be rejected in front of his friends he made a bet that he could sleep with her before the end of the year. He had become her perfect guy. Spouting all the things girls want to hear and being the overly attentive boyfriend. But at the end of the year when they were supposed to fulfill the bet she had not shown up. She had ghosted him.

When he was telling the story I couldn't help but smile at the fact that this girl didn't let him do that. That she had been smart enough to keep him from winning that bet. Never would I have thought that I would be falling in love with that girl. That his bet was now keeping my girl from loving me. From loving anyone really. Including herself. That was what pissed me off the most.

We had not spoken to each other in over two years. I had no clue what he was doing. I assumed he was still in New York. Living on his dads money and his name. Not giving a second thought to the girl that he completely broke.

And even after all that Vionette had given herself to me. But I knew it was not fully. I knew that she would not give me her heart. At least not yet. And then there were times like this morning. When her head was in the pillow she thought I was gone, but she heard me cough and I could see the smile that lit up her face. She may not want to admit it but she was falling for me too. I could see glimpses of her heart melting but then she would immediately erect another wall. And it was all because of him. I hated him. I wanted nothing more than to punch him in the face until he apologized to her. Maybe I would even let her punch him a few times. I had experience that she could throw and land a good punch.

I was smiling thinking about kicking the shit out of him when the familiar ring of my phone pulled me from the delightful daydream. Assuming it was Max or a member of the press calling about the restaurant launch Friday I just hit the little green button.

"This is Will."

"Hey man."

"Why the fuck are you calling me?"

"Dad told me that you bought him out and I wanted to wish you congratulations dude. That is a big dream of yours. Glad it's working out. I was also calling to tell you that I was gonna be in town for the opening."

"You're coming here? This Friday?" Thoughts of making my

dream a reality already started forming. If he was coming to me then I could settle this once and for all. I could feel the old me starting to creep up. I didn't just want to hurt him. I wanted to kill him. To rid this world of a dick like him forever.

"Actually I will be there Thursday morning. I have some business I need to take care of. Maybe we can get together Thursday night. Bring Max. We can do boys' night like we used to and y'all can show me what New Orleans has to offer."

"There is a restaurant near bourbon street. I'll send you the address. Meet there at 6?"

"Sounds great man. I am looking forward to it. There is a lot to catch up on."

"There sure is." I hung up the phone and I could not help but smile. Nettie would not get her revenge but I could get it for her. I would make sure that Matthew Price never ever used a woman as a game ever again. That was the least I could do. Nettie deserved better. She deserved the fucking world. And while I may not be able to give her that I could give her the heart of the man who broke hers.

Chapter 24

Vionette

All morning all I can think about is how I was going to get away without Aunt Margie knowing where I was going. I knew at some point I would have to tell her. But I wasn't even sure I would get the job and if I didn't then I would not have to tell her anything. I finished unloading the last of the new candles when I heard the doorbell of the door.

"Hello. I will be right with you."

"Take your time Darling."

That voice.

I smiled the biggest smile that I think my face muscles can make. But quickly toned it down before rounding the corner. Will was standing there in gray shorts and a muscle shirt. Holding flowers and a good luck balloon. He was sweaty but just the right amount making him smell like heaven and hell at the same time. I wanted to jump in his arms and kiss him until the worries that were in my head were completely forgotten.

Just his voice immediately relaxed me. I felt safe with him. I don't know how I knew but I knew that he would never hurt me. I knew he had a past. And he was far more experienced in almost everything in life, but here he was. Holding flowers and looking at me like he would devour me whole. And I was starting to think that I would let him. Not only that I would let him but I would enjoy every damn minute.

I walked to him and he placed the flowers on the counter, and wrapped his arms around my waist. "How do you feel about public displays of affection?"

"Normally I am not a fan. Most people go too far with it. I don't want to see two people playing tonsil hockey with each other. But it seems like I am changing my mind on some things that I used to not like the idea of."I met his gaze and he pulled me in tighter.

"So if I kiss you right now would I need to duck after?" He smiled and it lit up the room. And my heart melted a little bit. I was falling for this guy. I was falling for this guy hard.

"That depends on how good the kiss is." I lifted up onto my tip toes and allowed him to press his lips to mine. It was the perfect amount of pressure and teasing. How one man could be both so dominant and so gentle at the same time was still a mystery to me.

We continued to kiss until a cough behind me brought us both back to the fact that we were in public. "Really have to stop meeting like this Mr. Williams. I take it the restaurant is almost ready for Friday since you have time to stop working and buy flowers and a 'good luck" balloon in the middle of the day."

My heart dropped to my toes. Was she going to ask about it? This was the moment I had been dreading. Maybe though her finding out like this was better. Just rip the band aid and break her heart and then go to the interview and not get the job and then no longer have a job here either.

"I must say I hoped to receive an invitation to the opening but it seems that mine was lost in the mail." She laughs at her own joke but stares Will down waiting for a reply.

"My apologies. I had sent Max over to invite both of you but I guess he only delivered one of the invitations. Of course we would love to have you join us. After all it is a night for the 'who's who' of New Orleans. And you are certainly part of that list. I do hope that you can make it." He finished the invitation and then looked back at me not holding Aunt Margie's gaze but cementing his eyes to mine once more. "You are still coming also right. I mean I am sure we will have something to celebrate."

"And what are we celebrating?" Aunt Margie swiftly looked back and forth between me and will. He looked at me and gave me a slight nod and turned me slowly to face her. I closed my eyes and took a deep breath. Here we go. Get ready for the water works.

"We could be celebrating because I have an interview. Charlotte got me an interview with the editor at the publishing house. It's only for an assistant position but it would get me in the door. I have been racking my brain for how to tell you. I don't want you to think that I am not grateful to you Auntie because I am so so grateful.

I was terrified to break your heart or ruin your dream of us running the store together and then one day taking over. If you hate me I understand." I could feel the tears starting to sting the inside of my eyes. My breathing was heavy and while the armpits of my tank top was dry 8 seconds ago, I could fill a medium sized kiddie pool with the amount of sweat that had just collected there.

I could not look her in the eye. It all just came flying out. I had heard stories that people tell when they almost black out when they have to tell someone bad news.

I don't think I breathed for what felt like hours. I closed my eyes to try and keep the tears from spilling out. I don't want Will to see me so vulnerable. I realize how stupid that sounds as he literally took my virginity less than 24 hours ago but this was a different kind of intimacy; one that I was not ready for. Not yet. Maybe not ever.

I stood there for ages waiting for the tears to come. Both hers and mine. I felt the lightest touch on both sides of my face. I thought at first the hand belonged to Will, but they were soft and wrinkled. His hands were callused and covered my entire cheek. I slowly opened my eyes and I saw familiar gray blue eyes looking into mine. They were not crying. They were not pinched in heartbreak or anger. No. The thing that I saw looking back at me was love.

"Vionette Rachel Boudreaux. You listen to me. I am so honored to have had the privilege of caring for you these past several years. I was not fortunate enough to have my own children so you were an answered prayer. I miss your mother every single day but I will always be in her debt for leaving me with this precious gift. And yes I had hoped that you would take over the family business. But you are not gonna stop being family if you want to pursue your own dreams. No matter what you do I will be proud. Don't ever feel like you cannot follow your dreams. Do you hear me?"

Tears were expected from this conversation but tears of happiness were definitely not. "Are you sure Aunt Margie?

If I get the job I won't be able to work here anymore. Who would you get to help you?"

"You let me worry about that. You just worry about acing that interview and spending time with your fellow. In fact, take the rest of the day. Besides, if the last few months are any indication of the 'rush' I should be fine on my own."

I gave her the biggest hug and before breaking away I softly said,"Thank you Aunt Margie. I love you!"

"I love you too, sweet girl. Now go get that job."

I left the store with my flowers and confidence shining. I had told her and she had been proud. Not only did I get her permission but I had her support and encouragement to pursue not just this dream but any other that I may have. I looked down at the hand that was holding mine and I could not help but think that he was turning into one of those dreams. Was it possible that I was actually going to get my own happily ever after. No. Too fast Net. Calm down. You have to actually go to the interview first.

Just as the words entered my brain a loud growl came out of my stomach. I looked up at the face attached to the hand that I was getting very accustomed to holding and lifted one side of my mouth. "Apparently I should have eaten more of that delicious food you brought me instead of getting distracted. I should probably grab a quick bite before the interview. Would not want that noise to come out during the 'Tell me what is your greatest weakness' question."

"Fair. Wanna go to the diner or I do know a quiet little place where there is always good company and great food. The dress code is a little radical but I think you will like it." He smiled the same crooked smile that I did.

"Oh yeah. And where is this magical place that I have never

heard of before? And is it even open? I mean it is only 10 o'clock in the morning."

He pulled me into his arms fully this time and his lips hit mine with all the passion of a fire consuming a forest and when he broke apart his eyes were nothing but lust. He smiled that predatory smile that I had come to love so much. He bent over just enough so that his lips brushed the edge of my ears and whispered, "My place."

****

We crashed into the door. It was unlocked so I made a mental note to yell at him about the kind of people that lived in that area and that it wasn't safe and all that other bullshit. He kicked the door closed and we continued to explore each other with our mouths and our hands. We landed on the couch first. I don't know when it happened but my shirt was on the floor and he was taking off my shorts. He lifted my butt with his fist and slid the shorts down the rest of the way. Luckily I had felt sexy and put on the only sexy pair of underwear besides the ones I wore the night before.

"Black is definitely my favorite color. I was gentle with you the first time Darling. But now that I have tasted you I don't think I will be able to hold back this time. I need to hear you say okay. And as before if I do anything that is too much just say stop."

He was breathing as if he had just finished a marathon. Looking me over like a lion would look at a zebra. "I don't want you to hold back Will."

He grunted and was on top of me. Much more frenzied than before. And his hands were everywhere at the same time. In my hair and around my neck. Then on my breast creating the most exquisite sensations. He kissed me for a long time and then moved his mouth onto my neck. He bit and then sucked and I could see why the whole vampire obsession was a thing.

There were so many sensations happening it was almost too much. Everywhere that he touched there was heat and arousal was flooding me. His lips eventually found their way to my left nipple and I could not help bucking off of the couch. I moaned loudly and he mirrored the sound. He moved further still and I could not help the breath that hitched as I felt his hot breath close to my center.

"Wait. I have been moving boxes and sweating. I should probably shower before you do that. I am not one of those girls that glistens. I sweat and I am sure that it's a swamp down there."

"Net, there is no way that I am stopping from tasting every single inch of you right now. Besides,". He smirked again. "Flavor is what makes the meal right."

Holy. Shit.

He moved down before I could protest further and I screamed at the pleasure he was already wringing from my body. How could he know exactly where to touch and when to tease?

I could feel the volcano starting to rise. My body was doing things I had no clue it could do. Just when I thought that this was the pinnacle I felt him slide two fingers inside me. I erupted. My muscles rippled all over my body. I could feel myself tightening around his fingers. But he never slowed. After he wrung out every last gasp of pleasure from me he rose to be on top of me again. I was not sure what he was going to do and I was so drunk from the orgasm that I didn't care either. I couldn't open my eyes and my body felt too heavy to move.

"Open your mouth darling." I did so without question and he placed two fingers inside my mouth. I instinctively placed my lips around them and sucked. The taste was different. Like nothing I had ever had before. It had a hint of floral and pineapple. The more I sucked the more I actually liked the taste. I started to open my eyes and ask what that was but he answered before I could form the sentence.

"I didn't think it was fair that I was the only one with the pleasure to taste you. Now you know that you taste divine. And do not ever have to worry about that ever again."

Fuck. That was me. And damn if I didn't taste good. He was making me celebrate myself as a woman for the first time. I was no longer that girl crying in the rain in the doorway of a bar. I was a woman worthy of love and good things. I was a woman capable of giving love and receiving it. I was brave and broken and passionate and wanted. I was sexy and desirable. And this man had taught me all that. But even better, he had allowed me to learn it on my own. This man that had never been on the radar. This man who cooked with only veggies but loved to eat BBQ. This man who could read my body like a book and knew just what to say when I needed it. This man melted my heart of ice and started it pumping again. I smiled at him.

"My turn." I moved from underneath him to kneel before him. I started to undo his belt and his pants. He leaned back and allowed me to do it. His eyes were soft and sharp at the same time. I stared at him as my hands continued to remove the only barrier keeping me from my goal. And that goal was to give him as much pleasure as he had just given me. To let him feel what he was making me feel.

Alive.

Wanted.

Worthy.

I removed his pants and boxers. He leaned forward and removed his shirt with one hand. Only breaking eye contact long enough to pull it over his head. I moved my hand up and down his length. His eyes got heavy but he didn't close them. I gripped a little harder, loving the way he responded to my touch.

It was so easy to get lost in his face. His body. His responses were like gasoline on a bonfire. I continued to move up and down. I lifted just enough to be just over the tip of his length. I opened my mouth and a small amount of spit slowly slid out of it to land on the head of him. I followed his eyes and he followed that drop.

"Fucking Hell Nettie. Where have you been all my life?"

"Waiting." As soon as the word left my mouth I closed my lips around him and pulled him as far as I could take him. I felt his hands go into my hair and grip. Not hard but hard enough to warrant a moan from me.

"Do that again Darling, " he said with a growl.

So I did. I took control and moved up and down. I continued to use my hands and tongue. Alternating between tasting and sucking. His hips bucked with every swipe of my tongue on the head of his dick. And his moans were becoming faster and more insistent.

"God Baby, I am not gonna last much longer." The words were a pushed whisper. "Your mouth is too good and I can still taste you on my tongue."

I stood up and without saying a word I straddled him and

dropped onto his cock. Taking every single bit of it in one motion. We both gasped and he pulled me close, his lips closing on my nipple. I bounced and loved the way that it made me feel. I could feel the waves of pleasure building again. Apparently so could he.

"I want us to come together. Are you ready?"

"Yes. Yes please." I was able to inhale one time before the most beautiful crash of ecstasy washed over me. I heard myself moan as if I was watching the whole scene. I could see us. Our bodies molded together. It was almost hard to determine where he started and where I ended. A perfect fit. I opened my eyes and he was still resting his head on the back of the couch. I looked at his face and I could not help the tears that started to fall. Tears that I had been holding onto for a very long time. Tears that had made me give up on love. Tears that were caused by a man. These tears were also because of a man.

Not just a man, no this was my man.

I decided looking at his face as his eyes opened slowly and our gazes met, that I would tell him exactly how I felt after the interview. I was amazed that I was even thinking about this. But more than that, I was amazed that I had not had a panic attack after thinking about the interview. For the first time in a really long time I was excited about something that was mine.

Chapter 25

Will

This woman was starting to be a problem. I was not the romantic type. I saw what love did to people with my own parents. They loved each other more than life itself but they hated to be around each other. My memories of my parents were that of parties and and arguments.

"Why do you stay Mom if you hate him?" I had asked her this question so many times.

"It would be so much easier if I could hate him dear. Unfortunately that is not the case. We like to think that we get a choice in who we love but the only choice that we actually get is if we are going to submit to that love."

My mother was the wisest person that I knew. When she was not slurring her words they always held so much truth in them. I had remembered this conversation we had on the porch of our Texas home. My father was not a bad guy but was not the most caring either. His one true love was his bottom line and where his next million was coming from? He loved my mother at one point I know and sometimes I would see glimpses of that love. But they never stayed long. I remember thinking to myself that I would never let myself fall in love. I would never let someone have that kind of power over me. I would never hurt someone intentionally. Men who used women were the worst kind of filth in my opinion. But I could be honest with them and make sure that they knew that I was not the relationship type.

But one punch from Vionette Boudreaux had changed all of it. I not only thought about letting her have power over me but I welcomed it. She was starting to make me think about things I never dreamed I would ever think about. I had never spent the night with a woman. I had always excused myself for business reasons. I never brought girls to my place. It was easier to make a clean break going to theirs. I certainly had never woken up and made a woman breakfast.

With Net though I found myself wanting to take care of her. I actually wanted to know how her day was. I wanted to hear all about her ups and downs. I wanted to know everything about her. The good and the bad, although I was once best friends with her bad.

I found myself looking for a reason to be near her. When she left for the bookstore I immediately started thinking of ways to see her again. To kiss her again. I knew that she would be nervous about work and just as I thought it a balloon went flying past my window. I decided to get her flowers and then a silly balloon. She seemed like the kind of girl that liked sappy gestures of love. Seeing the look on her face when she saw me unleashed a new side of myself I didn't know existed. I loved seeing her smile. I loved how she looked at me with such joy.

I loved the way her lips melted to mine. And how our bodies just seemed to fit without trying. Holy shit. I loved her. I was in love with her.

I realized it while I was watching the exchange between her and her aunt. I knew it when she held my hand and we walked across the parking lot. I knew it when her stomach made that adorable little noise telling me that she was hungry and that I had yet another way to prolong our time together. I knew it as I did everything I could to make her body sing and rid her mind of anything and anyone that was not worthy of her time. I knew it when she tasted herself on my fingers and didn't shy away when I saw the realization on her face of what she was doing. And if there was any lingering doubt at all it faded completely when we both climaxed at the same time and I saw her looking at me. I saw my own feelings reflected there. This must be the sex brain talking. I loved her body and what it did to mine. I loved sex with her. There was no way this was real love. People don't fall in love in two weeks.

I made her a sandwich to eat on the way back to her apartment. So she could get ready for the interview. She kissed me and said she would call as soon as it was over. I told her that we would celebrate tonight with dinner. She had protested of course seeing the nerves starting to resurface. So I pulled her into another kiss, this one with a little more promise. "Being in the business I am in I have learned that not all celebrations are because of good news. Sometimes it's just because you are happy. And I hope that you are Nettie. Happy I mean. You deserve nothing less than that." I watched her face as she digested what I had said and she looked up at me and the smile that spread across her face almost made me say fuck it and pull her back in and say to hell with the interview.

She could work with me forever so she would always be near. But I knew how much this meant to her, and I wanted nothing more than to do whatever I could to make every single one of her dreams come true.

What the fuck was happening to me. I was becoming one of those guys that people on Tik Tok made fun of. What were they called? Oh, simps. I was a fucking simp and I think I liked it. Max was going to have a field day with this.

* * *

I got back to the restaurant around 12:30. I looked down the street waiting to see if Vionette would pass by on her way to the interview. But knowing her she was sitting in the waiting room already on the chance that she could be late. I walked in the door and was met with a frantic Max.

"Where the hell have you been? I have been calling you for three hours. Do you remember we have a restaurant opening in 3 days. Or did that slip your mind since you have been more occupied with sampling the local cuisine?"

I punched him hard, right in the jaw. I saw it in slow motion but I could not do anything to stop it. I heard his jaw crack. I just stared at him in disbelief.

"What the hell man? What was that for? If anything I should be the one punching you in the face. You have left me here to deal with all of this alone. I get she is hot but Christ Will. I need you here also. Or did you forget that we no longer have the backing of Matthew's dad." He got to his feet and rubbed his jaw.

"If you insult her again I will punch harder and longer. Get me. I am sorry for leaving you to do it all. But I am not sorry for punching you for insulting Nettie." And I helped him up. But I held his stare to make sure that if the punch wasn't enough the death look would solidify the threat was real.

"OK. OK. I am sorry. You know I would never say anything about her. It's just all the stress and you went and fell in love and now there is way more pressure on this place doing well and I cannot handle it man. I'm freaking out. How are you not freaking out?"

"What did you just say?" My blood ran cold. I started to sweat again. I needed to sit down.

"About me being stressed or you being all calm and cool?" He looked at me confused.

"Neither. The other thing you said about me being in love." I could barely say the words out loud.

"Oh that. Yeah man. I am sorry that I insulted her. I know that you love her and I would never do that to you. I respect the hell out of you. And by default Nettie. Although I think I would respect the hell out of her either way! She is awesome, and you are a lucky guy. I wish some of that would rub off on her friend."

"You think I love her? Like really love her?"

"Dude, when was the last time you surprised a girl with flowers and a balloon? When have you ever bought a girl a balloon?" He chuckled a little bit. "I have never seen you act this way and I have known you for the last 10 years. What did you think it was?"

"I haven't really thought about it." Lie. Total lie. That is all I have been thinking about since last night. And here was the answer with a bruise on his jaw. It was easy to rationalize the feeling away but when someone else is saying the same thing, that is harder to ignore. Especially when he had the evidence to back it up.

"What am I supposed to do now?" I was starting to feel the panic rising in me.

"What do you mean? If you love her then you love her and see what happens. If you are wanting me to tell you what to do then you are going to be very disappointed. I don't think I have ever felt even close to that. Well maybe. Possibly. But we are talking about you. I think it's pretty simple. You have to ask yourself a question. Do you love her? From movies and such I think you can tell by how much you want to spend time with them. Or when they are not with you, you start counting down the minutes before you are together again. Or like when you are not with them you see things everywhere that make you think of them. And it's the most random thing. Like a shoe in a shop window or a smell of a woman that passes you who wears the same perfume." He looked as if he was thinking of someone himself.

I took a deep breath. My mothers words came flooding back to me. Love was not the choice, the choice was power, and I had always maintained the power. Even when I was making it seem as though they had the power, i made sure that I stayed in control. But I had given power to Nettie. Both willingly and unknowingly. It just came naturally. trusted her. And all the things that Max had said about counting down till we can be together and making excuses to see her, were all true. I had done all of those things. So there was only one answer to his question.

I took another long breath and like an addict speaking at his first AA meeting said, "Yeah. Yeah man I love her. I love her so goddamn much. What the hell am I going to do?"

"Well first you're gonna stop freaking out. Although it's nice to know that you are human and have the ability to freak out. Then you are gonna help me get this place ready for Friday. You're gonna wait for your girl to call and tell you she killed it at the interview and then you are going to take her to a fancy dinner to celebrate and you're gonna put your big bro panties on and tell her how you feel!"

"Yeah OK. Sorry about leaving all this to you. That was a dick move. But it looks great. Have we received all the RSVP s?"

"I think so. And the staff is ready. I did get one unexpected RSVP though."

I knew exactly who he was fixing to say. And I could feel my body language begin to change.

"Matthew Price called and said he was going to be in town for his dad and wanted to stop by and celebrate with us so I told him the details. I asked how his old man was taking being fired and he just laughed, sounded a bit creepy but he always did have a little psycho streak. Especially with girls." Max started to turn and I grabbed his arm harder than I meant to but there was no stopping the rage that came from me.

"That bastard is not to set foot in this restaurant. Do you understand me?" I stared at him like he was my mortal enemy and not my best friend. I waited for him to say something but he just looked confused.

"What the hell man? Where did that come from? What did he do to you? Did he cuss you for firing his dad?"

"No. He didn't do anything to me nor will he do anything to me or mine ever again."

"Dude why do you sound like one of those 'touch her and die' book boyfriends right now?"

I let go of his arm. I didn't realize I was still holding it. I turned around and ran both hands through my hair. If I didn't tell him then he would never understand but I knew how personal this was to Nettie. I also knew that if I told him he would not see Matthew in the same way either and while I could give two fucks if Matt ever had a friend again, I knew Max would be just as protective of Nettie and he isn't as good at at controlling his temper as I am.

"Do you remember that story that Matt told us about the girl at school that all the boys thought was hot but she would not give any of them the time of day? And so they made that bet and the night he was supposed to close the deal she broke it off?"

"Yeah man. How could I forget? That was wrong even for him. Why does that have anything to do with now though?" His look of confusion was both innocent and infuriating and I had no clue why it was making me so angry.

"Well the girl was Nettie. He dated her for almost a year. Played her left and right and then she found out about it and broke it off before he could seal the deal."

"Fuck me dude." I recognized the same shock that I had felt and then just like me I saw the rage in his eyes. "I'll fucking kill him. When he comes to the launch we will jump him in the alley. There are crocodiles right. We won't ever get caught."

"Death is too good for him. No, we will make sure that he and Net are never in the same place. He doesn't know that we know anyway. I just want to protect Nettie from ever seeing him again." It did feel like we were planning a murder and in a way I guess we were. Not in the physical sense but Matthew had become dead to us both. And Net would never have to go through that again. Never.

Chapter 26

Vionette

It's odd. I never would have thought that today would be the day that changed my life. You always hear people say "the day started out like every other day." Mine had started with me thinking the best night of my life was a dream. Until I heard his voice and knew that it had not been. He was real. The memories were real. And what I was feeling for Dillon Williams was very real. He had shattered the wall that I had placed on my heart in a matter of a few weeks.

Growing up in a book, you are hit over and over with the idea of the damsel in distress. I had promised that I would never be that girl ever again. However, now I am looking at those stories through a new lens. These women were never helpless. They had what they needed the whole time. They just needed someone to push it out of them. Cinderella needed a stepmother who was a raging bitch to make her realize she deserved better, and she deserved to dream. Belle needed the beast to show her that she could have a relationship with someone who would see her for the person she was and not the role forced upon her. Will was my push that I needed. He had made me see that I was capable of big things and that I deserved big things in return.

Those dreams were necessary to live a fulfilled life and so was having someone to share that life with. When I closed my eyes it was his face that I saw in the morning. It was his voice that I wanted to hear throughout the day. It was his arms that I wanted to fall into at the end of a long day and get lost in the warmth of his smile and his body.

I was stirred out of my daydream but my phone gave the bird chirp that I had a new message.

"Good luck today. I know that you will do great! Cannot wait to see you! And wear that floral top with navy pants. You will look amazing in it! Later girl."

I had one hour. One hour to get the smell of Will off me. One hour to find the right outfit using Charlotte's rules. One hour to fix my hair, get dressed and change my entire way of thinking. One hour. HA!

I had wanted this so much for so long. When you are faced with everything you have asked for or dreamed of you start to question everything you have ever done. And that is what I found myself doing. I finished the shower and then put on a simple pair of dress pants and a pink floral top. The sleeves were slightly puffy but the color highlighted my hair and my skin tone. The pants were a nice deep navy color that brought out the navy in the flowers. I decided to do a bohemian braid for my hairstyle. Simple but fitting the vibe of the outfit. I paired it with some simple wedge heels and grabbed my bag and walked out to my Uber.

I passed the same landmarks that had been passed a thousand times on my commute. The same trees whispering in the breeze. The benches with homeless men and women trying to nap or make a little money with instruments and their own voices.

When I passed the bookstore my heart lurched. I had been given her approval. Not only her approval, Aunt Margie had given me her support. But I could not help the guilt that hit me as I passed in the car, that I was doing something wrong. It felt like the trip was happening in slow motion.

When the car stopped outside the editors building, I froze. Was this a mistake? Could I actually do this? What if I didn't get the position? Or worse yet..

What if I did?

I opened the door and walked inside. The lobby was beautiful. All white and creams with splashes of color in the artwork and the furniture. I walked up to the receptionist desk. Before I could say my name I was met with "Hello. You must be Charlotte's friend. Vionette right? I will let Angela know that you are here. Can I get you anything while you wait? Water, tea, coffee? Anything. Also I love your top. You and Charlotte have great style. She has helped me so much with my own these last few months. Oh goodness I'm rambling. I do that. Oh and I am Mandy. Just let me know if you need anything while you wait. Okay."

She was everything I wanted to be. Tall. Slender but curvy in the right ways. Her hair was the most brilliant shade of auburn where mine looked a little dull. Her eyes were piercing green and her smile was as white as porcelain. I could see why she was the first face that you met when you walked in the door.

I looked down at myself and immediately questioned the choice to come here. Looking around at the few others that worked here I didn't look like any of them. I had some sense of style and I knew that I wasn't ugly by any standards but these people were on another level.

"Vionette? You okay? I've been calling you for a while. Angela is ready for you. Good luck!"

"Oh okay, Yeah sorry. I'm ready." Lie. I was not ready at all. Not even a little bit. I had made a horrible mistake. This was the mantra playing in my head as I walked into the office of Angela Fields. What was I thinking?

"Please come in Ms. Vionette. I am just finishing this email and then I am all yours." I was confused. The picture in front of me didn't match the picture in my head. When I pictured Angela Fields I pictured someone a little more, well, more. I had thought about her as the Miranda Priestly type. Very elegant and regal almost. That is certainly the vibe that the others around the office had.

But the lady in front of me looked more like…me. She was wearing a loose fitting sundress and a jean jacket. I could see under her clear desk and she was actually wearing white vans. Her gray brown hair was loosely braided to the side almost mirroring my own and her glasses were a bright green color. She had a huge smile on her face as she typed that made me feel immediately at ease, like a long lost aunt.

"Okay. And done. Hello, I'm Angela Fields. Lead editor and finder of stories untold. And you must be Vionette. Charlotte has spoken so highly of you for so long. I hate that we have not had the pleasure of meeting sooner."

"Thank you. Charlotte speaks highly of you as well, Ms.

Fields."

"Oh we are not that formal here. Everyone calls me Angie. You are welcome to do the same. Now the position is an entry level assistant. I would need you to help answer phones and handle my schedule. There would also be some entry level editing. You would get the manuscripts and weed out the ones that you don't like, then pass on the ones you do to me. And always get yourself a coffee if you get me one. Pay is minimum but I think it's fair. I just want you to know what I expect before we go any farther. So does this sound good so far."

"Good. Oh um yes. That sounds great. Thank you."

"Great. So I know you like to read so I will not insult your intelligence by asking what brought you here. I am in the business of telling stories that have never been told. So Miss. Vionette, what is your story?"

"Oh please call me Nettie. Or Net. My story. Oh um. Well, I graduated from The University of New Orleans with my English lit degree with a minor in Editing and Journalism." As soon as I started to speak she looked down and then cut me off.

"No, not your resume. I want your story. I want the part that makes you you. What are you scared of? What makes you smile, cry, laugh? What has shaped you to be the woman you are today? That is the story that I want you to tell me."

"I mean I am not that interesting at all."

"Why don't you let me be the judge of that. Now go."

I channeled all of the rambling energy that I had been fighting and let it fly.

"I came to live with my Aunt here in the city after my parents died. I have worked in her bookstore for the last 5 years but have looked at the doors of Fields Publishing wishing I had the guts to interview. I had my heart broken by a boy in college who made a bet with his friends that he could get me to sleep with him and take my virginity. But I found out about it and swore to never let a man get close to me again. I was doing so well until I met Will. Dillon Williams. He is opening a new vegetarian restaurant next to the bookstore. I have been in love with his food since I saw a piece in a magazine about him but he was a ghost. We met at a restaurant where he tried to help me home and I punched him in the nose. Then he stalked me and made me go on a date with him. Then he called me while he was away and gave me the best orgasm of my life over the phone. He surprised me and flew back yesterday and we made love all night. So not a virgin any more. He brought me flowers and a good luck balloon this morning and we had sex about two hours before I came here. He makes me smile and laugh and makes me cry but in the best way. And it scares me because he doesn't scare me at all. The only thing that scares me is that he may not feel the same but I think I saw it in his eyes. The same look that I have when he is around. Like he is what makes the sun shine and colors beautiful. But that cannot be right. Love like that isn't real. It's just in books, right?"

Angie took a deep breath and then leaned back in her seat. She placed her glasses on the desk in front of her and folded her hands in her lamp. I could not read what that stare meant. But I had just told a prospective employer about my sex life with a total stranger so the odds were not looking good. Honestly that was probably for the best. I could go back to the bookstore and continue just like I had for the last 5 years.

"Can you start next Monday? The hours are 8-5. And please wear what you are comfortable in. I have no clue why everyone in this office feels like they need to dress so formally all the time." She was leaning on the desk now with an envelope extended to me with what I assume is new hire paperwork.

"What? You are hiring me. Even after all that I just said? Why?" I waited holding my breath, knowing that she was just pranking me. I don't know why but she seemed like the type that would get a kick out of that sort of thing.

"Net. I am hiring you *because* of what you just said. In this business you have to have an eye for a good story. Not the ones that are well written or look the part. But the ones that make you feel something. The ones that you can relate to and that others can relate to. The reason I ask that question is to see if you can find the elements in your own story that make yours relatable. I want to know more of your story. I want to know what happens to the guy in college. I want to know your Aunt and see the bookstore. But most importantly I want to know what happens between you and this guy. You pulled me into your story. That is exactly what we do here. And you have a talent for it. Maybe leave out the bit about the mind blowing sex next time though."

"Yes ma'am. I would be honored to start on Monday. Is a skirt and tank too casual?" I was smiling so big that my cheeks hurt.

"That is perfect. See ya on Monday. Just bring that paperwork back then. And welcome to the team, Nettie. Oh and good luck with this guy of yours. I look forward to hearing how that part of the story ends."

"Me too."

Me too.

****

I got it. I actually got it. I was the new assistant to the editor of

Fields Publishing. I had called Charlotte the second I left Mrs. Fields office. Wait, Angie. She said to call her Angie. I could hear her scream on the phone and in real life. Honestly, I didn't know she could scream like that. More for the point of her being an actress. I then took a breath and called Aunt Margie. I knew that I had her support but saying that she wanted me to pursue this and then actually telling her that I would be leaving were two very different things.

It rang a few times and then, "Hello. This is Margie Boudreaux. How can I assist you on this fine day?"

"Hey Margie it's me. Nettie. I just finished the interview. I have some news."

...

...

...

"Well, girl what is it? Did you get the job? Did they fall in love with you like I knew that they would?"

"Um, kind of yes. She wants me to start Monday. Is that okay? I know it's short notice and I can always decline the offer if I need to." I could feel my panic settle over me but before it had a chance to take root I heard a soft breath inhale and then exhale.

"Vionette. Rachel. Boudreaux. You are named after the most successful women in our family. Your great great grandmother, your great aunt, and me. Each of us made our own way from nothing more than an idea and a strong work ethic. And you will be no different. You will start Monday and you will do your best! You get coffee better than anyone who has ever gotten coffee before. You will assist better than anyone has assisted before and then you will become an editor yourself and then will have to hire another brilliant young girl that just needs to see in herself everything that those around her sees."

God, how I loved this woman. She could make me feel like I could conquer the entire world with one hand tied behind my back. I was overcome with relief and love and encouragement. Excitement started to bloom in me that I had not felt in a long long time. Was I actually getting everything that I want? The job of my dreams and Aunt Margie's approval and support. The guy that was almost too good to be real and he actually was choosing me too. This didn't happen in real life. There was always a catch, a 'not so fast' moment that crushed the protagonist before they actually got everything they wanted. That is the way every single story lined up.

"Hey Nettie. I hope that you haven't forgotten my offer to meet Thursday. I really would love to talk about how things ended with us. I'll be waiting at the diner. I hope to see you there."

Well there it is. The catch. If I met him would I be able to see past his hurt and betrayal. Why does he want to talk now after all this time? Oh God, maybe he is dying. Am I a big enough bitch to deny a man his dying wish to make amends? No, I was the new Nettie. The new me was not scared of meeting with an ex and hashing things out like an adult. I could do this. He could not hurt me anymore. No one could. I hope.

Chapter 27

❧

Vionette

I clicked on the icon with his name and the message opened fully.

"Hey Nettie. I hope that you haven't forgotten my offer to meet Thursday. I really would love to talk about how things ended with us. I'll be waiting at the diner. I hope to see you there. I don't want there to be anything unfinished between us, especially now."

Oh shit. He was dying. Why did that make me sad? I hated him. Hated him with a passion of a thousand enemies, but I didn't want him to die. Well I did at one point. Prayed for it actually. Crap did I do this. Had I given him cancer or something? Well now I have to go and see what he has to say. Damn conscious. It could not be that bad right. We are adults now and I have a great guy. It will be fine.

"I will meet you at the diner at 1:00." Easy. Simple and to the point. I could do this.

****

After that message there was one other person I needed to talk to. I took a deep breath and pushed all the old memories out of my head and clicked "Not vegetarian Chef" and waited.

"Hello darling. I was just thinking about you. You were wearing my favorite dress and I had you bent over a very large desk with papers thrown all over the floor. You were mad but my tongue and fingers quickly made you forget that. How was the interview? Will we be celebrating two things tonight?"

"Two things? What is the other thing?"

"So you got the job?! I knew you would. How could they not hire you! And yes I have some news. But it can wait till tonight. I will be here helping Max for the rest of the afternoon. I have been a shit friend and he has carried the load for the last few days. Apparently I have been distracted. I cannot imagine what could have done that?"

He chuckled and it went straight to my core. How did this man do that with just his voice? I didn't even have to be near him to be totally affected by him.

"Hum. Nope. Cannot think of anything." I loved flirting with him. "But I am sure if you think about it real HARD then something will COME to you."

"You're killing me. I need to stay and help Max but if you keep talking like that then I may just have to fake getting sick and take the afternoon off."

"No, don't do that. You have been a shit friend, and the opening is in just three days. Stay and help. I will meet you tonight for dinner. And maybe we can get through an entire meal before we rip each other's clothes off?" I smiled on the phone hoping he could hear it in my voice. God I loved flirting with this man.

"OK. I will leave a little early and pick you up around 7?"

"No. I will meet you there. Take your time. Hang with your friend. Besides, I will need to go shopping to find just the right dress for celebrating the new Vionette Boudreaux."

"Oooo. Sounds intriguing. Well, you know what color I will say to pick. Looking forward to seeing what you pick. And then seeing it on the floor or ripped into pieces." He growled the last bit just a little and I felt his voice in all the right places.

"I'll see what I can do. Until then."

"Until then."

****

I decided to see if Charlotte would like to meet me and shop. I knew that sometimes she was able to get out of the office early if she had completed all her tasks.

"Hey. So I was thinking about going shopping for a dress for tonight and for Friday. Are you available?"

"Is that even a question? I will be there in 10 min. Are you at your house or the store?"

"Neither. I am still right outside. I was afraid to leave. I am still in shock. So I have been standing here for the last 30 min. I know. I'm crazy."

I could hear her take a long breath. "You are not crazy. You are alive. And that is both amazing and scary as hell. But I am so fucking proud of you! See ya in a few."

I smiled. I smiled at myself. I smiled at Charlotte. I smiled at Will. I smiled at the way these last few days have played out. I was on the brink of getting everything I had wished for. The job. The guy. The confidence. There had been a time when I wanted all of these things and more. I thought I was getting them with Matthew. But he just showed me that happily ever after didn't exist.

Then these two mystery men from New York show up and I am believing again. So much so that I am terrified. I thought this was all a made up thing but here I am. Waiting for my best friend to help me buy a dress to tell a man that I think I am falling in love with him. Who am I?

I am Nettie. New assistant to the head Editor of Fields Publishing. Former bookstore clerk to the best Aunt in all of New Orleans and the lover of a brilliant vegetarian chef. I am the girl I have always wanted to be.

I see Charlotte coming to the door and I blink and she is standing next to me. I can smell her perfume and she is smiling at me with that stupid grin she does when she is truly happy. And I cannot help but think to myself how much I owe this woman.

"Hey bitch. You ready to spend all your hard earned money? What kind of dress are we looking for? Easy access I assume?!" She winked at me when she said it. And I laughed from my toes.

"You guessed it. But it has to be black."

"Done and done. Let's go. I know just the place. They won't know what hit them after we are done. I hope you brought another pair of shoes in that suitcase you carry around."

I reached into my bag and pulled out my white vans. "I got it covered. Charlotte Piper. Do your worst. Make me over like they do in the movies. You know right before the dance when the frumpy girl takes off the glasses and puts on some mascara and suddenly she is the prettiest chick in the room. I want that."

"Well, you are already that, but you had me at makeover. Let's do this!"

She started typing away on her phone and before she walked ahead I saw her making an appointment at a hair salon near the boutique. This was going to be a long afternoon. But it had been a long five years also. I was ready for this. After today I would not be the people pleasing girl that never went after what she wanted. I would be the girl who walked up to the hottest guy and kissed him like no one was watching. I had a plan now.

Get the job. Check

Get the dress. Check

Get closure with the douche. Pending..

Get the guy. Also pending. I still didn't really know how he felt about me.

Get my happily ever after. If it even exists?

Yep things were falling into place. What could go wrong?

Chapter 28

Will

I had been sitting at the restaurant for about 10 min. I had gone over what I would say to Net when she arrived about a thousand times. I even did the cliche thing where you talk in front of a mirror and role play. If the me from 15 days ago could see me now I would kick my own ass.

I had helped Max and we talked a little more about love and what to do. He mentioned having a similar problem but would not tell me with whom. Although if I had to guess, I would say it was Nettie's best friend, whats her name.

He had given me a pep talk right before coming here tonight. I stopped and bought a large bouquet of yellow and red roses. Net didn't seem like the classic rose girl. She seemed like she would like purple but the small florist didn't have anything like that. So I went with a classic with a twist. Just like my girl. Damn, I liked the way that sounded.

I had ordered a bottle of champagne once I received the

text that she was on her way. I was starting to look over the menu when I heard the tale tale ring of the door and my heart stopped. No it didn't stop. It exploded.

Holy.

Fucking.

Shit.

Standing in the door was not my girl. No, this was Aphrodite herself. I looked her up and down like I was going to be tested on her every inch, and I would gladly take that test. She had always been beautiful and sexy but this was a new level.

She wore red heels that made her legs look even more incredible than they already did, showing off her running figure. Her dress was sinful in the way that it hugged her every curve. When she moved her arms there was a tiny mesh peek a boo slit down both sides from her arm to her thighs on both sides. The dress only made it to the top of her knees. Her hair was slightly shorter, with a 'recently fucked" curl to it and it seemed a little more red than it was this morning. She wore minimal makeup but had bright red lipstick. I immediately thought about how the color would look wrapped around my hard cock.

She was radiant and confident and sexy as hell. She walked past a bus boy and he dropped his tray. I would have to punch him later for that look but I could not blame the guy. Every single guy that she passed glanced at my girl and some of the women. She was the most beautiful thing in this place, hell, in this city, and she was looking at me. She was smiling at me.

"Hey handsome. Are you waiting for someone?" Her eyes were pure lust and happiness. There was no way that I was making it through an entire meal without ripping every inch of clothing off her body. I wonder what the fine would be for having her right now on this table. I smiled at the mental image.

"Well, that depends maim. Are you looking for someone?" I smiled the smile that I knew she loved and leaned into the table closer to her. Shit she smelled amazing. Vanilla and spice and sex.

"I am. Tall, dark and handsome. Successful. And great in bed. Know anyone like that?" She giggled a little. I liked this new Net. She was confident and it suited her so well.

"Well I don't know about the tall, dark and handsome bit. But if you are looking for someone great in bed, I have never had complaints before. I can give you references if you would like."

"Oh well, aren't you cocky sir. Maybe let's just see how the night goes." She laughed again and then leaned over the table so that our noses were only a few inches apart and said, "I hope you like the new look. I wanted to surprise you. I also wanted to give you this…" She closed the distance and gave me the most earth shattering kiss I had ever had. I stood and brought her closer, not caring in the slightest that we were in public or that the entire restaurant had stopped and was watching our interaction like a movie.

We broke our kiss when the waiter returned and coughed. "Would you like to hear the specials for tonight sir?"

I removed her from my lap and stood. Walking her to the other side of the table with my hand placed in the small of her back. I remembered that last time my hand had been here in a restaurant. I pulled out the chair for her, tracing her neck with my fingers and placing all of her hair onto the left side. Noticing a small tattoo that I had not seen before. "Yes please. Thank you."

"Well we have a lovely braised pork and new potatoes. And for the adventurous type we have a spicy craw-fish curry over wild rice and asparagus. We also have a.."

I could not focus on what he was saying. I was too distracted by the living dream in front of me. If I had any doubts about how I felt about this girl they went crashing to the ground along with my heart. I was caught in her spell. That is the only way I could describe the change that had come over me; magic.

"Will, what sounds good to you?" Her voice pulled me from the daydream playing in my head.

"Um, I'll do the pork. And for the lady.."

"I will do the vegetarian curry please. Thank you."

"Of course. Let me know if you need anything at all. My name is Justin." He said the entire speech looking only at her. And who could blame him.

I handed him the menu and thanked him again. Then I focused all my attention on the girl in front of me. But she was no girl. It was like she had grown up in the last 6 hours. She was a woman. A confident radiant woman.

"You should be ashamed of yourself maim." The corners of my lips lifted slightly as I said the words.

"Oh and why is that?"

Her lips did the same. She knew exactly what she was doing. Fuck me.

"Well we are supposed to be celebrating you and the new job. But now I will have to spend this entire dinner, not celebrating, but using every ounce of control that I possess to not put you on this table in front of all these people and rip you apart in the best way." And it took all my self control to finish that sentence. I knew sitting at that table, the way that she matched my flirting and my teasing. The way that she had never backed down from a challenge from me and how her body language seemed to instantly relax when we were together. That I loved her and that she also cared for me.

"Poor baby. Well, there is a solution."

She moved her chair closer to me. I placed my hand on her inner thigh. My fingers started tracing small circles along her legs until I reached the hem of her dress, noting how high up her thigh I had to go before reaching it. I heard her breath catch for a moment and her gaze went from lust to pure heat. She slowly uncrossed her legs under the table. An invitation. That is what this was. And invitation to appease my attraction and longing. She slowly leaned into me and whispered, "I am also having to fight taking you under this table. But it would seem that we are in luck as this restaurant has a tablecloth and shields anything that may or may not be happening underneath. For example, no one would know that you are a finger's length from seeing just how much I want you. And no one would know that I am not wearing anything under this dress so if you wanted to check for the evidence yourself then there would be nothing to hinder that investigation."

Yep. I am a goner. Shit.

"Well if it's for science." I slowly traced my fingers up her inner thighs, remembering the soft skin that had been wrapped around my head, and just as she said she was already dripping for me. Her breath caught briefly as I slipped two fingers into her wet center. I could not help the growl that slipped past my walls of strength. I saw the waiter bringing the drinks and so, reluctantly, I slid my fingers from their warm embrace and saw the frown that immediately replaced the ecstasy on Nettie's face.

"We will have to continue this later, darling. It seems the

service at this place is top notch." I smiled the roguish grin that I knew she loved. And the smile that she answered it with was purely magic. "Vionette, I have something that I want to tell you. I think, no I know that I am …."

"Would you like me to place the wine in a decanter for you so that it can breathe for the evening sir?"

"Um, no that won't be necessary. Thank you."

We watched him open the bottle and then place it on the table after pouring each of us a glass. It was like watching a movie in slow motion.

"Will, I have something to tell you also. I think that we may have to be more intentional in planning our dates from now on. Seeing as I wont be right next door for you to just come over anytime you want. Max already texted me that he would need a period of mourning for not being able to annoy me whenever he wanted. So I was thinking, would you maybe want to move in together? I know it may be fast but I think we are a good fit and I would like to see where this thing goes. What do you think?"

This thing.

This thing?

Is that how she felt? That we were just a thing? Well, if that is how she felt then maybe telling her that she was my entire world and that I was completely and totally hers in every way and that there was not a single cell in my body that didn't love her needed to wait. Besides, maybe this was the more mature way of doing this. I was a practical man after all and this was good. Slowing it down a little. I think I fell in love with her more for the idea. She was trying to protect both of us. She had given me her body but it seemed she had not yet given me her heart.

The rest of dinner consisted of forks scraping plates and conversation that never seemed dull or forced. We talked about her interview and how the other women who worked there didn't match the editor at all. We talked about Nettie's mini therapy confession but I didn't feel like she told me everything about it. We talked about how the restaurant was coming and that we only had one more inspection before we were given the green light to open. I mentioned that I would not be available Thursday as the inspectors would be coming at some point that day but we didn't know exactly when. She said OK and that she had plans anyway so it was fine.

Once the food was eaten and I paid the bill, there was electricity in the room. We had stolen touches all night and it was clear that we both wanted to finish what we had started under the table.

We made it to the door and before I could say anything, "So handsome, your place or mine?"

I laughed. A real laugh and said, "Ladies choice. Although I do think yours is closer. How long are you willing to wait for me to finish what we started?"

"Mine it is!"

I pulled her in for a small kiss. But that kiss held all the promises of not just the evening but of what we could become together. I was starting to see a future with her and with my hand on her lower back walking her to the door I realized the only future I did see was her. I had not thought about the restaurant this whole time. I had not checked my phone or my watch. If this woman was in the room I was totally devoted to only her.

Shit. That scared the hell out of me.

I could hear some hesitation on her part during the night

even in asking me to move in together. I sensed that was more of a precaution than a declaration of feelings. In fact she had not one time eluded to having feelings for me. At least none that could not be sated with a few careful movements of my tongue.

Was I falling for her more than she was for me? I mean she had asked to live together but she hadn't said she loved me or even that she liked me. I knew that she loved what I could do in bed but she had not one time said or mentioned anything about feelings. What was I doing?

Chapter 29

Vionette

Dinner was amazing. But with Will everything is amazing.

The next day went on as it usually does. I worked at the shop to get everything ready for the college student that would be taking my spot. Apparently, The University was looking to expand their work program and they contacted Aunt Margie and she agreed before the lady could finish her speech. I would be training the new girl for the next few days until I started my new position at Fields Publishing.

Charlotte and I went shopping that afternoon for our opening dresses. Hers was positively sinful and I couldn't help but overhear her saying "Eat your heart out douche-bag" as she tried it on. Mine was as if it were made just for me except it needed to be hemmed a little bit. But I felt confident and sexy in it. I was feeling more of both of those things lately. The haircut and makeover I am sure have something to do with it but also something else. I was happy. Truly happy. I was seeing a future that I was in charge of for once in my life, and that future looked pretty great.

I just had to get through one more thing and then I could fully give into the feelings that I was having for Will. I could see that he liked me a lot. But I still didn't think it was fair to truly tell him how I feel until getting closure with *him.*

Speaking of, he was sitting at the table right in front of the restaurant. The one where anyone passing by would be able to see. I didn't want this to be a show. I certainly didn't want Charlotte to walk by and see much less Will. He seemed the jealous type and I didn't want to see that side of him. I have a feeling that his "not nice" guy side would be in full view.

This lunch was about me. About letting go and finally being able to move on. Or that was what I was hoping to be able to do.

I walked in the door and the chime alerted everyone that someone new was here. I turned and our eyes met and in one look I was right back where I was 5 years ago. Scared, devastated, betrayed. He looked exactly the same. A little bigger in the middle and his clothing was a little more grown up but those eyes, that smile, all the same ones that promised me so much and then only delivered heartbreak.

You can do this Net. YOU are a strong confident woman. YOU are starting a career. YOU have a bad ass best friend who got you an amazing job with the coolest publisher ever. YOU have found a great guy and he treats you well. And YOU have you. He cannot hurt you. He won't hurt you. Never again.

"Wow. Nettie. You look incredible. All grown up I see. And I love what you did with your hair. It suits you." I could hear how nervous he was. His voice cracked a little in the last sentence and I could see sweat stains in the armpit of his shirt when he stood and moved my chair. "Who would have thought we would be here again after all this time, huh?"

"Yeah. Who would have thought. Why are we here Matthew? I made it very clear that I never wanted to see or talk to you again. So why now are you calling me out of the blue to meet? I have a theory but I am sure it's not right." I crossed my arms and glared at him.

"Oh. And what is your theory? I would love to know. Truly. I can only imagine what it could be."

"Well I think because you are a horrible person that does horrible things, God finally got it together and gave you cancer or some awful disease that You are now dying from. And now you are trying to write your mistakes like those steps you do in AA. Am I close?"

He looked at me and blew out a long breath that I didn't notice him take while I was talking. Defeated. That was the only word I could come up with to describe him. His shoulders slumped in the seat. It was like I had punched him in the stomach and all the air in his lungs had been shot out.

"I deserve that. I am so sorry for all that I did to you. I was the most vile person ever and I will never be able to fully make up for the hurt that I have caused you. I am in fact not sick or dying. At least not that I know of. I am however making a big change soon and we don't feel right starting out with unresolved issues in our past."

We? "We?"

"That is why I asked you to meet. I am getting married in October. She is amazing. Found me at a horrific time in my life and helped stitch me back together. She is the one who showed me what a disgrace I was to you and also who showed me that for me to fully give my heart to her, I needed to apologize for breaking yours. Or at least try. I am so very sorry for how I behaved toward you and while I know that total forgiveness is way more than I should ever ask for or deserve. Maybe a truce would be OK. We are thinking of moving just outside the city and one of my college buddies is opening a restaurant this Friday. So we may be seeing each other a....."

"Wait, who is opening a restaurant?"

"An old college buddy of mine. He went to culinary school and I came here for business. His name is..."

"Dillon Williams?"

"Yeah. Have you heard of him? Of course you have. You are a vegetarian and that is his specialty. My dad used to finance his place but he stormed into the bank and cashed in his trust and then fired my dad out of the blue a few days ago. I called Max to congratulate him but I guess with the stress of the opening he hasn't returned my call. I was hoping to surprise him at the opening tomorrow."

I could not breathe.

Will knew Matthew.

Matthew knew Will.

They were friends.

I told Will his name and he never said a word. Not a single word.

Then I remembered his change of demeanor when I told him the name and his abrupt leaving after.

"That was your dad he had to deal with after I told him about you. He went to Dallas to fire your father. So that I would not have to see you or be near you ever again. And he didn't invite you to the opening because I would be there and he was trying to protect me. And now I am here with you face to face to hear your apology so that you can live happily ever after with another woman?"

The laugh that escaped me was borderline insane. Every single person that was in the bakery was looking at me. I could not control it. I laughed until my stomach hurt and my cheeks burned.

"Did I miss the joke?" He looked confused and worried at the same time.

"No. No. I am sorry Matthew. I am sorry that I believed you all those times you said you cared. I am sorry that I was naive to think that a real man only cares for his success. I am sorry that I allowed you to have so much from me all these years. And I am truly sorry that you felt you needed to apologize to me. Once upon a time I felt like I needed and deserved that apology. But I no longer do. I forgive you. I hope that you find happiness with this girl and I hope that you treat her like she deserves." I had been laughing through the whole thing.

I stood up and after I caught my breath, walked over to the other side of the table. I gave him a hug and I think I meant it. I was free.

I was free of the hurt. I was free of the pain. I was free of the control and power that I had allowed this man to hold over me without even knowing it.

And I was free to tell the man that I love that I was his totally and completely. For the first time in five years I was in charge of my own life. I had gone after the job that I wanted and gotten it. I had been honest with Aunt Margie and had received her support and pride. And now the only thing left was to get the hunk. I was no longer concerned with what others would think or if others would like my choices. I didn't give a damn about others. All I wanted was my piece of happy. And I knew just the guy I wanted it with.

I picked up my phone and hit the button that would connect me with said person. It rang and rang and no answer. I guess he was busy with the last minute things. We had not made plans for today just in case and I was excited to see him tomorrow at the opening. I could show off my new dress and my new outlook on life. Gone was the Vionette that could be controlled. This was a new day. A fresh start. And I was finally ready to give the man who had tamed my body to submission the permission to do the same to my heart. It was his from the first time we kissed. And this meeting with Matthew did nothing but confirm it.

Why else would he have left and bought out Mr. Price. Why else would he have made it harder for himself and Max. Why else would he have been so tender and understanding if he didn't care for me? I loved him with every single cell in my body and I was confident that he felt the same. Well pretty confident. I guess I will find out tomorrow.

Man I wish this was the day after today!

Chapter 30

Will

The plates were washed. The napkins pressed. The menus are bound and ready. The staff was as trained as they could be with no one to wait on. The food was immaculate and delicious. There was a buzz in the air when I walked the floor one more time before opening. It had come together better than I had hoped. My best friend came walking from the kitchen. My sous chef and partner. He was not dressed in his cooking attire.

No tonight would be about mingling and meeting the big wigs of the town. Tonight was about the impression. Tonight was supposed to be about new beginnings in all aspects of my life.

"Well buddy. Are you ready for this? I mean I know you have done so many of these but this is the first one with only your name on the line. No going back now!" Max tapped me on the shoulder. He looked good in his suit. He looked the part of a successful restaurateur. Gone was the kid needing to prove something. Here was a man ready to conquer the world.

"Yeah man, I think I am ready. Thanks for all your help. Especially with me losing my head there for a bit. I promise it won't happen again."

"No worries man. I am kind of glad you were distracted. It gave me the push that I needed to really see if I have what it takes to do this. And I think I do. Really. I may even like the set up more than the cooking. How crazy a turn is that." he smiled from ear to ear. Happiness. This was real happiness but I could not help wishing that he had someone other than me to share it with. He deserved it.

"That is an unexpected turn. I hope that wasn't also your resignation?" I looked at him with both humor and worry on my face.

"Naw man. I could never leave you. Plus if I leave the eye candy goes way down and we cannot have that before we get our Michelin Star." He waggled his eyes and smiled even more. I couldn't help the relief that I felt.

"Are you getting your girl for the opening?"

"No. We decided to meet here. I have a surprise for her that I wanted to give her at the party. She agreed saying she could use the extra time to get ready. Her and Charlotte should be here soon." I noticed a slight cringe when I spoke of the beautiful best friend of a certain someone that took over Max's face. But I didn't push it.

No, I needed to save my energy. I did in fact have a surprise for Nettie and it was walking in the front door.

****

The party was a hit. There was laughter and smiles. There were empty plates and happy faces all around me. The who's who of

New Orleans had shown up and shown out. I could not have asked for a better opening. The mayor even stopped in and gave us a plaque. Apparently, She had gone vegetarian a few years ago and hated that there was not an upscale vegetarian place to dine at. She had pushed for the permit to be approved. I told her that she was welcome anytime and we would love for her to be the first to try out new dishes.

I was speaking to one of the staff when the door opened. And it was as if the entire world stopped. First the leggy blonde that walked in would have any man fall to their knees on the spot. But the goddess behind her would make entire empires bow.

Nettie had chosen a navy blue dress. Not a dress but a gown. It was the color of the sea where it drops into the abyss. It fit her like a glove in all the right places and it hugged her curves so that I knew that every man would sell their soul to have a chance to touch her. There were no straps and it made her breast look so enticing all I could think about was what it would feel like to slip my hand under that bodice and caress the nipples that I knew would be pebbled underneath.

She made her way to stand beside me and I had to remember how to speak. Because when she stood next to me, gone was the feeling of want and lust and in its place was only that of betrayal.

"Well, I would love to meet the man responsible for all this. He must be a real catch. Hiya Handsome. The place looks amazing!" She reached to place her arms around my neck. But I faked a sneeze to keep her from touching me. I knew that if she did I would no longer be able to give her the surprise and I was so looking forward to the look on her face when it was revealed.

"I hope you aren't getting sick. I would hate for that to spoil your big night." She looked at me with actual concern.

As if she actually cared for me.

As if she wanted what was best for me.

Now was as good as any to give her her surprise. I held her hand and took her to the front of the restaurant. I let her go and motioned to Max that the time for the speeches was here. He smiled and walked to join me. I looked back at the girl in the blue dress and smiled.

"Ladies and gentlemen. Thank you so much for this reception. My business partner and I could never have imagined this when we started talking about moving to New Orleans to open our own place. But here we are and here you are making it a success. Thank you for allowing us to become a part of this community and for all the support that you have shown." I intentionally took a pause and stared into the eyes of the most beautiful girl in the world and said, "And it is with that being said that I must announce I will be heading up a new development in New York, and I am leaving this in the capable hands of Max here and our newest partner, Matthew Price. We reconnected just yesterday and I pitched the idea to him over dinner and he accepted."

As soon as I said his name, Matthew strolled from behind the kitchen door and stood next to Max. I looked back at those beautiful green eyes and saw confusion and worry.

"Thank you again for all that you have done, and I hope that you will all show these men the same level of acceptance as you have shown me. I am sure they both will be in capable hands." I made sure to look right at Nettie for that last bit.

Confusion greeted me back.

The crowd cheered, and I was met with congratulations and

well wishes for my new adventure. I fought the crowd and made it to the door and into the night. Where I was greeted with the sounds of the city and a voice that dimmed it all.

"What the hell was that?" She was confused.

"What was what, darling?" I turned and looked at her, trying to pretend I had no clue what she could be confused about and the look on her face almost crushed my resolve.

"That little speech. When were you going to tell me that you were leaving and that you were working with Matthew?"

"When were you going to tell me that you were also 'working' with Matthew. I saw the two of you in the deli. I saw you laughing and then hugged him. I saw it all Vionette. Let me see if I can guess what happened. You ran into each other like some romance movie. He told you that he was moving here and you just couldn't wait to jump back into his arms. I'm sure his game has improved over the years. After all, he already knows all of your tales and just the right places to get you….Fuck!"

Once again my nose was acquainted with Nettie's right hook. I could taste the blood filling my mouth and running down my chin. I was right back in front of a restaurant, having been hit in the face by her.

"Holy shit, Net. What the hell!"

"I had to do something before you ruined your chances at everything in front of you. Jesus, Will. For as intelligent as you are, you're a real dumb ass. And you have no clue what happened. Not that it is any of your business, but Matthew did contact me. He wanted to apologize for all those things he did. He wanted to make amends, so that he could start fresh with his new fiance. He told me that they are moving here and that he knew we would run into each other and his fiance wants to make sure that we could coexist in harmony or some shit like that. What you saw as me laughing was me finally realizing that he didn't deserve my time and he never did. You saw me finally let go of all that hurt so that I could tell you with an open mind and a mended heart that I love you. I could not wait to tell you after I talked to him. I am sure he left just as confused as you were when you saw us together. I even called you when I left to tell you to meet me sooner so that I could tell you everything and show you just how much I had let go of everything holding me back from giving all of me to you. Not just my body, but my mind and soul and most importantly my heart. So again, when were you going to tell me that you were working with him and that you were leaving?"

Shit. I had messed up. I had royally messed up.

"I contacted him after I saw you walking away. I told him that I had been approached and since he was not his father, I would be interested in seeing if he would like to work with Max and me. I said it was because I was trying to be a good guy, but the truth is, I was only making sure he would be at the opening to hurt you. I wanted you to feel the way I did standing outside that deli, seeing the girl who had totally ruined me for all women, laughing at the man who ruined my chances of being able to capture her heart. Of showing her that she was the most confident, amazing, successful, gorgeous woman on the planet and the only one that could not see it was her because of one douche-bag. The same douche-bag that she was hugging and smiling at. I saw red and my old ways came crashing in on me. I don't have anything else lined up. We did have dinner Thursday night and he told me everything. Confessed to Max and me which I have to say made me respect him a little bit. He wants to get away from his dad and this was a way for him to do it. I was going to start looking for something tomorrow. I promised that I would never fall in love. Dillon Williams doesn't fall for the girl. He doesn't give over control. Or at least he didn't. I didn't. Not until you."

I finished and stood in front of her. Nose bleeding like a stuck pig and panting, trying to stop the tears that were rising to the surface.

She looked back at me and then started to turn around. She walked through the door back into the restaurant. She was lost in the crowd for about 5 min. She then made her way back to the door and stepped back outside.

Walking right up to me, she stood toe to toe and looked me dead in the face. I sucked in a breath without realizing that I had, and she noticed it also because a slight smile hinted at the corners of her mouth. She brought her hands to both my cheeks and forced my eyes to lock with hers, blood already staining her hands.

"You are not looking for some other project to start. You are staying here with your best friend and new business partner. It will be weird but you can handle it. You are not leaving New Orleans. You have built something amazing here and you need to see it through. And you are going to kiss me and tell me that you love me. Because I love you too, Dillon Williams. I have loved you since that first kiss at the deli. You brought me to life and showed me that I deserved a life that was full of love and goodness and so do you. Do I make myself clear?"

Those tears that I tried to suppress were flowing freely now. She loved me. Really loved me. And God, did I love her back. We could do this. We would do this. I looked back at her and simply said, "Yes, Darling. Loud and clear."

She grabbed my face harder and pulled me to her, planting

a kiss right on the mouth. We broke apart and her face was smeared with red, but neither one of us cared. She was the beauty who had needed someone to show her she was worthy of everything good and beautiful, and I was the beast who needed to learn that power given to the right people could be amazingly freeing.

She linked her arm in mine, and together we walked back through the door. To our friends and family. And into our own love story as written by Vionette and Will.

Epilogue

One year later

Vionette

"OK. Can you have the final manuscript to me by 5 today? Wonderful. I look forward to reading it." I hung up the phone and looked at the clock on the wall. I had 45 minutes until this work day was complete. It has been a roller coaster of a year.

I started the new job and it was even better than I had hoped. I was reading the most amazing stories every week. I had made some pretty big discoveries, which led to me being promoted to junior editor in charge a few months ago.

I was offered to head up a new office in New York that I accepted. Hence the celebration that I was counting down to.

Will's restaurant was booming, making a name for itself in New Orleans, as well as neighboring cities and even states. Max had taken care of the kitchen to free Will up to handle the business side of things, and Matthew had started to learn the ropes to take over for Will. Turns out there is a big need for more vegetarian restaurants in New York after all. At least ones that are solely owned by Dillon Williams.

We were set to leave in a week. He had flown up a few times to find an apartment that was close enough to my office and an easy commute for him to the sites they were considering for the new place.

Finally the clock struck 5 and I gathered my things. I picked up my purse and made my way to the front doors only to see Charlotte waiting for me. With a small box in her hand and a smile on her face.

"Hey Char. I thought you left hours ago. What's in the box?"

"Oh, I did. And this. You'll have to open it to find out." She squealed when I reached for the small wooden box. I opened it and inside was a small fork. "What is this for?" I looked at her confused and waited for her to fill me in on the joke.

"I was told to give you this box. And then take you to the best vegetarian spot in town. Have any clue where that would be?"

"I do. But what is all this about? Did Will put you up to this? He is not the grand gesture type."

"Cannot say. I am under strict instructions not to fraternize. I am on official business." This encounter is only confirming my previous thoughts on her being a stellar CIA agent.

"OK. Then lead the way."

I followed my best friend around the corner and down a few blocks until the familiar street came into view. A street that had held so many memories and all the promise of the future. I walked past the bookshop that now was a thriving hub for the university students. I believe the latest review said something like "cool hippie vibes." Aunt Margie had sold the entire store to the university who now used it totally as a work study program.

The extra traffic had also helped boost foot traffic to the restaurant over the last few months. Not that it needed any help. But a little help never hurts.

I walked through the familiar doors with the owner's name displayed proudly. And immediately noticed that the lights were off. The evening rush would be starting soon and there should be people getting ready. At least the staff should be here. But there was nothing.

I looked around for a bit and then heard a door open behind me. When I turned, all I saw was a bouquet of balloons and flowers and legs jutting from the bottom of both. Laughter and recognition hit me at the same time as I noticed who the shoes belonged to.

He continued to walk to me. When he was finally within arms reach, I moved the balloons aside to look at his face. He was grinning from ear to ear.

"What is all this for? When you said we were having a party I pictured people, food, electricity. Not cheap balloons and depression. What's going on? Also why did you give me this tiny fork? Are you trying to tell me that I have put on weight cause I don't see you doing crunches in the morning mister!"

"Will you shut up, woman."

He put the balloons and the flowers to the side of him. He then grabbed my hands and with the slightest of sighs gave me a look that I swear went to my toes.

"Nettie. We didn't start out on the best of shoes. In fact, I think the ones I wore still have a stain of blood on them. We didn't do things in the order most people do them in. We are the least likely pair, with you being the naive bookworm and me the world renowned chef, all knowing and well traveled and …"

"Get on with it please." I laughed a little but I did want him to finish.

"Our love story is not one that you will find in a book or a movie, but it is real. And it is true. As for the fork, some people believe that because forks were invented by humans they represent our ability to create things with our minds rather than with just our hands; others believe that forks represent how we are able to take small bites out of something before eating all of it at once. I believe that they are the vehicle in which good things are brought to us. This fork brought you to me today."

As he finished the last words he slowly reached into his back pocket. He pulled out another small box. This one was a light blue color. He knelt to one knee and grabbed my left hand once more.

"I want to create things with you Nettie. I want to create a life with you. And I don't want to take small bites. I want to take big bites. I want to experience all life has to offer with you at my side. Marry me, Nettie."

"Yes. A thousand times yes!" I could not get the second yes out before I was being spun around the room. As my feet hit the floor the lights came on and out from the kitchen came every one of our friends and family. Charlotte standing next to Aunt Margie. Max standing with Matthew and his fiance, whom I actually really liked. The staff was finally starting to prepare for the dinner rush and the familiar sounds of the kitchen filled my ears.

I looked at all the people that I loved so much in this world. I looked at the man currently placing the prettiest ring I had ever seen on my hand. I could not control the tears that flooded my eyes and started to run down my cheeks. This was happiness. This was what the books write about. It had not been a "once upon a time" beginning by any means. A princess that was broken by a beast and a prince blinded by a notion that love is weakness not strength, but with each other, they learned that love is not an idea but a choice. A choice that you make every moment of each day until death do you part. As I looked at the faces of my favorite people in the whole world, I knew that it was shaping up to be a pretty amazing "Happily Ever After."

Author's Notes

As a little kid I wanted to write books. I was always a big reader and have started hundreds of stories. It was not until I found a local bookstore and joined a book club that I started to think that I could maybe actually do this. I kept meeting people that had either already written their own works or that were in the process of writing them. It was amazing and not at all lost to me that I was surrounded by authors.

So, when making my New Years resolution, I decided not to waste it on something silly like worrying less or loosing a few pounds, (thanks Tic Tok for making us big girls hot!). I decided that I would fulfill my dream of becoming an author.

This process was not at all what I thought it would be. I went into this adventure with a clear picture of what writing would be. I made an outline and downloaded all the things. But then I noticed that the characters came to life as I wrote them. And often times they told me what was going to happen next, outline (and my sanity) be damned.

I was met with adversity and critique and quite a bit of writers block here and there. But here she is. My finished book.

I hope that you like this book as much as I do. Happy Reading!

About the Author

Ashley McClure is a first time author. As a self-proclaimed book dragon, her favorite genres are spicy romance, horror, and Agatha Christie novels. When she is not writing, she is a teacher of little minds and big hearts. She lives with her daughter, husband and their zoo in Hoschton, GA.

You can connect with me on:

https://www.facebook.com/ashleymcclureauthor